BULLARD

OF THE SPACE PATROL

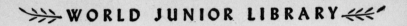

≫≫ WORLD JUNIOR LIBRARY ≪≪

Bullard
OF THE SPACE PATROL

by MALCOLM JAMESON

edited by ANDRE NORTON

CLEVELAND · NEW YORK

THE WORLD PUBLISHING COMPANY

Library of Congress Catalog Card Number: 51–12352

HC 755

·In gathering the adventures of Bullard and preparing them for the press the editor had the assistance of Martin Greenberg, who first introduced Commander Bullard to the editor's delighted attention, and Nan Hanlin, who loaned her precious Bullard adventures for critical reading. Deepest appreciation is hereby expressed to both.

· CONTENTS ·

BULLARD

OF THE SPACE PATROL

INTRODUCTION · *Navies thrive upon traditions and those traditions are man-made. Ancient luster still shines from such names as Jones and Barney, Hull and Peary, Decatur, Nelson, Drake and Hawkins, Lief Ericson and Ragnor Lodbrok. And behind these are other clever sailors from Crete and Phoenicia whose titles and distinctions may not have descended through the veils of history but whose methods and know-how certainly did.*

So are there also tradition-makers among the mariners of deep space—among the men and officers of that patrol which keeps the peace of the inner and outer planets, or wages the grimmest of all war in that black night where stars are suns and the slightest miscalculation means a death undreamed of when men rode sea water instead of interstellar vacuum.

John Bullard was a tradition-maker (and breaker, too, when the occasion demanded). He did not choose this unique position in regard to the Service; it was forced upon him by fate, luck, or whatever Power decides the future of space-roving humans.

There was nothing heroic about him to catch the eye or rivet the attention. He was neither six-foot-three with muscles to awe an envious Jovian, or a little Napoleon. He was neither handsome nor ugly enough to cause comment. He was reputed to be able to think fast in an emergency—but since that is an attribute demanded of

11

*all space officers, it did not distinguish him in any way
from his fellows.*

*Born on Terra, in the ancient district of Ohio, in the
year 3915, he passed in due course into the Patrol
Academy, where he was an average student, and graduated
into the Service standing about a third of the way down
his class. From there on he served the usual tricks in
various ships, gathering during that process the rating of
"competent" and the liking of those who knew him well
enough. (He was a quiet, rather studious youngster and
had few close friends.) When he passed from ship to
ship it was with the good wishes and favorable reports
of each commander.*

*In 3940 he had reached the rank of Lieutenant by
regular, steady promotion. And then came the affair of the
Admiral's Inspection and Bullard's real career began.
As it continued he showed that he was the stuff from
which such biographies as this are made. "Deep Space"
Bullard—maker of traditions!*

ADMIRAL'S INSPECTION

·How about a snappy round of meteor ball before we eat?"
"You know me," grinned Kingman, the torpedo officer,
from the cushions of the transom.

"Swell," said Fraser, gathering up the cards from his solitaire game. Fraser had charge of the auxiliaries and the mercury vapor boilers.

"How about you, Bullard?" Lieutenant Bullard was the latest comer to the *Pollux*. He had belonged to the mess too short a time for the others to learn much about him.

"Why, sure," said Bullard. He slid a marker into his book—*Hints on Ship-control, Star-class Cruisers*—and laid the volume carefully to one side. "Only I didn't know—" he hesitated, glancing in the direction of the executive officer seated in a wicker chair in a corner of the wardroom.

"In the *Pollux*, Bullard," spoke up the exec—Commander Beckley—"keeping fit is as important as anything else you do. If you're inclined to split hairs over the regulations, I'll ease your mind on that score. You are *detailed* to play. That makes it official."

Bullard reddened slightly at the implication he might be a sky lawyer, the bane of ships from time immemorial. But Commander Beckley was smiling pleasantly. He did not mean it that way; he was employing his own method of initiating his newest officer into the usage of the ship. It was true that officers were not supposed to leave a ship while under way, but notwithstanding the regulations, Beckley saw no good reason for making them forego their daily exercise. The *Pollux* was swinging lazily in a wide orbit about the Jovian System, her electronic blasts cold and dark, patrolling for routine traffic-control purposes. Forbidding men to go over the side was as senseless a restriction as to prohibit swimming from an anchored ship.

"I think some exercise would do me good, too," yawned Chinnery, chief engineer, stretching languidly. "Count me in."

Chief Watch Officer Moore, who had proposed the game, frowned slightly. That upset the balance; five made unequal teams and there was no one else free. He turned toward the exec with a question on his lips, but Beckley had leaned over and was clicking the intership phone, calling Central Control.

"CC? Put the O.D. on. Carlson? A little game of meteor ball is starting. They need a sixth. You're it. Climb into your suit and report to Mr. Moore on the port boat deck. I'll take over for the duration."

The phone was slammed down with a click. The exec looked up. "You had a question, Moore?"

"Why, no, sir. That is, thank you, sir."

"Half an hour," smiled the exec as he rose to go to Central Control to relieve Carlson.

Bullard glowed inwardly. What a ship! No wonder she was regarded as the happiest home in the sky fleet. Clean, taut as a bowstring, yet friendly. From what he had seen, officers and crew were like one big family. The discipline was excellent—but invisible. One could almost term it voluntary. In the few days he had been aboard, Bullard already sensed the difference between the spirit exhibited on this snappy cruiser of the first line and that on the obsolescent reserve mine-layer he had just left, but it took this incident to make him understand why. It was the difference in the personalities of those in control of the two ships.

He had no regrets now for leaving the old *Asia,* even if he had been chief engineer of her and here he was only a junior officer. As he recalled her meddlesome, old-woman-ish captain and the endless bickerings of the wardroom, he was aware he was glad to be well out of her. In contrast, the *Pollux* had Captain Mike Dongan, aloof and reserved, but capable and invariably pleasant; her exec, despite his air of geniality, held the ship to strict standards of per-formance; her wardroom officers, for all their pose of flip-pant indifference, were conscientious in the performance of their duties; her crew, in consequence, were fiercely loyal. All that together made for that prime essential of a "good" ship—esprit de corps—something a man could work for, fight for, die for. There was a new lilt in Bullard's stride as he hurried down the passage to shift into a lightweight spacesuit for the game.

He made his way to the boat deck, and as he stepped out of the air lock onto the broad fin he was impressed by the size of the huge vessel. Its hull sloped upward and away from him, gray in the dim light of a dwindled sun, and he saw for the first time the row of alcoves let into the ship's side that sheltered the boats. Those, he knew, were used for the reconnaissance of asteroids or areas too rugged to put the ship down on, or for minor searches, or for rescue ex-peditions. Star-class cruisers, being designed for all-planet service, were equipped with vertical and horizontal fins to stabilize them when easing into an atmosphere, and the horizontal ones made ideal landing decks for their boats.

Bullard saw that the other players were already gathered at the extreme edge of the fin and behind them two diminutive Ganymedean messboys were struggling with the squat sports-howitzer. As he made his way toward them they fired the first of the two low-velocity luciferin bombs, and in a moment, the two shells bloomed into pale green stars, several miles apart and several miles away—the goals for the game. By the time he had joined Fraser and Kingman on the right, the messboys were loading the mesothorium-coated ball into the howitzer. The game was ready to start.

At a signal from Moore, one of the Ganymedeans yanked the lanyard and the glowing ball was hurled out into space, squarely between the goals. In the same moment the six players took off, soaring in swift pursuit behind it, belching thin threads of fire behind them. Ten seconds later the sky to port and above was a maze of streaking, interlacing flames as the players zigzagged to and fro, intent on getting a grip on the ball long enough to propel it toward one or the other of the slowly receding goals.

Commander Beckley watched the fiery skylarking with keen interest. Meteor ball, he thought, as he gazed into the visiplate in CC, was the ideal game for skymen. It was good for the muscles, for although the player had no weight to speak of, he was compelled to put himself through continuous contortions in order to manipulate the flexible, bucking rocket nozzle and still keep an arm free to fend off tackling opponents or to bat the ball along. But far more beneficial was the ingrained sense of tridimensional orientation the game developed, and the capacity to appraise the reaction from the hand-jet impulses. That sense of action and reaction in time became almost instinctive, giving the player that quality so indispensable in the handling of spaceships —that elusive thing known as the *feel* of a ship. A man possessing that could, in a pinch, handle his vessel blindfolded or without instruments.

Twice Beckley watched a thin line of flame lash through the cool green blaze of the luciferin goal marker, other lightninglike flashes hard behind. That meant that one of the teams had scored twice—clever work for so short a time. And it was unusual, for although the Polliwogs had many good players, they lacked brilliant ones. Beckley correctly surmised that it must have been Bullard who scored the goals; the two officer-teams were too evenly matched otherwise.

He chuckled as he suddenly realized that now the Polliwogs might snatch another trophy from the Castor Beans, their traditional rivals on the sister cruiser *Castor*. He reached for the long-range televise transmitter on the impulse to call Warlock on the instant and challenge his gang to a game the very next time the two ships fell in together, but as he turned away from the visiplate he noticed the men in the control room silently stiffening to attention. The captain had come in.

Beckley was astonished at the gravity of the skipper's

expression, for so far as he knew, all was serene. But at first the captain said nothing. He merely looked thoughtfully about the control room and, seeing his exec in charge and no officer of the deck, he glanced at the visiplate.

"Sound recall," said Captain Mike. "Then read this."

At a nod from the exec, the man on the signal board closed a key. The wailing buzz it set up in the helmets of the officers flitting about outside would inform them they were wanted on board with all dispatch. Commander Beckley took the proffered signal from the captain's hand and glanced through it, noticing that as he did, Captain Mike was watching him stolidly, giving no hint of what was in his own mind.

"Yes, I saw this," said Beckley. "What is it, a joke?"

"Joke!" snorted the captain. "Apparently you have not heard of the outcome of the *Canopus'* inspection. Do you realize that Joey Dill has been relieved of his command and stuck in the dark on Uranus for a five-year hitch as commandant of that flea-bitten outpost? That every one of his officers is awaiting court-martial on charges ranging from 'gross inefficiency' to 'culpable negligence'? That the *Canopus*, herself, is practically a wreck and has been ordered to the sky yard on Mars for survey and wholesale repairs? There is nothing funny about that. And now it appears we are next."

Commander Beckley stared again at the innocuous-looking message in his hand. It still looked like a prank fathered by someone on the admiral's staff. It read:

From COMMANDER JOVIAN PATROL TO CO POLLUX:
You will be in readiness for General Efficiency Inspection 1400 SST 14 May 3940 Terrestrial Year. Entire personnel Castor will inspect in accordance with Archive Reprint USN-1946-FT-53.

ABERCROMBIE.

"Unless I'm crazy—and I won't admit it," said Beckley slowly, "this says that we will be inspected by the crew of the *Castor*."

"Yes." The captain's eye was gleaming.

"And if that is not joke enough, it goes on to say that they will do it according to some aboriginal practice or other. Shades of Hanno and Nelson! What did they ever do on a trireme that is applicable to us?"

"The principles of warfare change very little through the millennia," remarked Captain Mike, dryly, "and, moreover, your history is a bit foggy, Beckley. The Phoenicians much antedated the Americans. The latter were far more advanced. As a matter of fact, they are credited with the invention of the first spaceship. In any case, our admiralty commission, that has been digging through the records unearthed in the excavations for the fifth sublevel at Washington, has decided that some of their practices were good enough to be reinstated. So there we are."

"Meaning, I take it, that we are to be inspected according to some system invented by John Paul Jones, Sims, Leahy, or some other long-dead old seadog?" Beckley was thankful he had remembered the names of a few of the early Terrestrials. It was a polite rebuttal of the skipper's comment on his historical knowledge.

"Exactly."

"All right," said the executive officer. "In that case, I will get ready. In fact, we're ready now. You know inspections never gave us any worry."

"We've never been really inspected before," was the captain's grim retort. "Step down to my cabin and I will give you a copy of that reprint."

Ordinarily, the commander would have greeted the returning ballplayers with some jolly pleasantry, but although he saw them trooping in, gay and ruddy from their brisk workout and the bracing showers after it, he said not a word to them. He was deep in the perusal of the antique document exhumed from the vaults below the old city of Washington. The deeper he read, the faster his confidence in the ship's readiness oozed away. At first he had some difficulty with the outmoded terminology, but as he groped his way through it, glimmerings of the immense difficulties before him began to appear.

In the end he sat in astounded admiration at the ingenuity of a people he had long thoughtlessly regarded as primitive. Small wonder their ships had behaved so well during the great Terminal War of the Twentieth Century. The marvelous stamina they displayed was due to the fact they were prepared—prepared for anything, whether accident, damage in action, or catastrophe of nature. So long as any craft of that age remained afloat, its crew continued to work it and to fight it. And now he had learned why. *They knew their stuff*. The system they followed forced them to. Hence, the admiralty's recent adoption of that system.

Beckley sat through supper very quiet and seemingly morose. He was engaged in appraising himself—Chinnery, Moore, Fraser, and the rest. How good were they, for all the trophies they had won? He remembered wryly how they won first place in the acceleration contest. He and Chinnery knew that the circuit-breakers were lashed down and every fuse in the ship jumped by heavy copper cable. He and the surgeon knew how heavily the men had been doped with *gravonol*. It had taken four days of special rigging to accomplish that feat. Highly artificial! Bah! It was an empty triumph, now that he thought of it honestly in the light of what he had been reading.

After supper, over the cigars, he attempted to convey to his juniors some of what he had just learned and what was ahead of them. It was not easy. The *Pollux* had for a long time been considered a model ship, and it was the conviction of most of her officers and practically all her crew that she could do anything any other ship could do and do it quicker and more smoothly than any other afloat in the ether.

"So what?" demanded Chinnery, as soon as he learned that for the duration of the tests, Pete Roswell of the *Castor* would be at his elbow, watching and noting everything he did, and that rating for rating, every man in the black gang would be matched by his opposite number from the sister cruiser. "Let 'em come. Let 'em watch. They'll learn something. Who cares what they see? My uranium consumption, acceleration for acceleration, is the lowest in the whole star-spangled fleet. We haven't had a breakdown of an auxiliary in more than a year, and that's a record for any man's service."

"That is just it," observed Beckley pointedly. "You're *too* good. It makes you cocky and you take too much for granted. What would you do if you did have a breakdown —cut in your reserve generators, I suppose?"

"Sure—always have. They work, too. Both sets."

"And if those went on the blink?"

"Well—there are the selenium units on the hull, only—"

"Quite so. Only there isn't much sun power out here by Jupiter and you haven't run a test on them since we left Venutian Station. But suppose you did hook 'em up and could get a little juice out of them and then *they* went out, what?"

"For the love of—why, storage batteries, of course."

" 'Storage batteries' is good," snapped the exec. "In the last quarterly report, if my memory is correct, they were listed as being in 404D, your space storeroom. How many amps do you think you could pull from there?"

Chinnery lapsed into a glum silence. He had never seen the exec in this mood. Beckley turned to Fraser and asked abruptly:

"What do we do if the intership phone goes out?"

"Shift to telescribes."

"And after that?"

"The annunciator and telegraph system."

"And after that?"

Fraser looked puzzled. "If we lose the juice on the annunciators they can be operated by hand." He shrugged. "After that, if you insist on it, there are always messengers."

"Why not voice tubes?" queried Beckley, cocking an eyebrow.

"Voice tubes?" echoed several. The others laughed. The admiralty *had* gone primitive.

"That is what I said. Believe it or not, gentlemen, but the *Pollux* is equipped with a complete system of voice tubes, gastight covers, and all. Yet not one of you knows it. You have probably painted them over, or stuffed them with old socks or love letters. Now get out of here, all of you, and inspect your parts of the ship. Come back at midnight and I will tell you more about this inspection and what we have to do to get ready for it."

The group of officers returned to the wardroom at twelve, not greatly enlightened by their inspection. They knew what the commander was driving at, but most of them felt they already knew the answers. On a warship there are always many alternative ways of doing the same thing, for in the heat of action things go wrong and there is no time for repairs. But most of them were already familiar with what they had to deal with, except Bullard, of course, who was new. He was the only one of them who had the slightest doubt of his readiness for any test that might be put to him.

Cracking jokes, but at the same time slightly mystified by the slant the executive had taken, they assembled. Commander Beckley entered and tossed the reprinted early-American document on the wardroom table. Moore crossed the room and fingered it, noting its title. It was "Chief Umpire's Report, Battle Efficiency Inspection U.S.S. *Alaska,* Spring, 1946."

"I have told you we are to be inspected by the *Castor,*" began Beckley. "What I didn't tell you is that later on, we inspect them."

"Whee!" yelled Fraser. "I've always wanted to know how they puttied up that main condenser. It is nothing short of a miracle how it hangs together."

A look of smug satisfaction flitted across Chinnery's face. In his estimation, Pete Roswell, engineer of the *Castor,* was a stuffed shirt.

Moore was smiling, too, the contented smile of a cat contemplating a canary. Freddy McCaskey, navigator and senior watch of the rival ship, was also his rival for the hand of a certain young lady residing in Ursapolis. His brilliant take-offs and landings in the skyport there had long annoyed Moore, for Moore knew, even if the admiral did not, that they were made possible by certain nonreg gadgets bolted to the underside of the *Castor's* chart rack. They were nonreg for the reason that they were unreliable —they could not be counted upon to stand up under the shock of action. Moore itched to be in a position officially to expose them, and by doing it burst the bubble of Mc-Caskey's vaunted superiority as a ship handler.

There were others present who had similar designs calculated to upset the peace of mind and complacency of their friendly enemies, judging by the ripple of anticipatory grins that swept the room.

Beckley's eye roved the group, missing the reaction of no one.

"Ah," he breathed, "so that's the way you feel? Well, let me tell you this—so do the Castor Beans. And don't ever forget, they inspect us *first*.

"But don't misunderstand me. There will be no cutthroat competition about this. Friendly rivalry, such as we enjoy with the *Castor*, or outright malice, if it were present, makes very little difference. The men from the *Castor* do not inspect us in the sense of passing judgment; they merely observe and record the data. It is the admiral who does the judging. But you can bet your bottom dollar they won't miss anything. They live and work in a ship the exact twin of ours, and they follow the same routine. They know our weak spots and how we go about covering them up, for they have the same spots and, I daresay, use the same tricks. We might fool the old man, but never a Castor Bean.

"As I said before, they will all be here, from Captain Allyn down to the landsman for cook's helper, and every man jack of them will have a stop watch and a notebook. We will be covered, station for station, all over the ship.

"Leaving out the preliminaries, such as looking at the

bright work and haircuts and all that sort of thing—which
worries none of us—the first thing that happens to us will
be the emergency drills. Those are going to be different.
The American doctrine was that the real test of an emergency organization is an emergency, and one peculiarity
of emergencies is that they come when you least expect
them. Moreover, the people on watch at the time are the
ones who will have to handle them. That means we cannot
hand-pick our best and most experienced men to do the
drilling.

"It will be worked this way. The admiral will ask to see
our watch list. He'll run down through the names and pick
one at random. It might even be Bullard, here—"

Bullard winced. He did not like that "even," though he
was only three days in the ship.

"And he will say, 'Send Lieutenant Bullard in.' Bullard
will have to relieve the deck. We may cruise along an hour
after that, not knowing what is coming, when suddenly the
chief umpire will announce, 'Fire in the lower magazine,'
or 'Penetrating collision,' or whatever emergency they have
picked. Every *Castor* man starts his stop watch, licks his
pencil, and looks at the man he's umpiring. The test will
be not only of Bullard, but of the whole organization. As
for Bullard, he is in sole charge, and neither Captain Dongan nor I can advise him, and the rest of you can only execute what orders he gives. Whatever he does, whether the
right thing, or the wrong thing, or nothing at all, goes down
in the notebooks, and also the manner of its execution.

"Let us say the conditions announced are that a small meteorite has penetrated the collision bulkheads and padding and has come into the crew's quarters. We are in ordinary cruising condition—that is, without spacesuits on. Were our interior gastight doors closed and dogged? If they were not, we lose air throughout the ship. Bullard, no doubt, would order a repair party forward. The *Castor*'s repair party will go through the intermediate lock with our party, noting everything. Did the lock work smoothly? What kind of patch did the repair party put on, and how long did it take? Were they skillful or clumsy? How long after that before air was back in the compartment? Did the patch leak? How much elapsed time between the alarm and 'secure'?

"You get an idea from that of how closely we will be supervised. I need not go into all the other emergency drills, or the possible variations on them. The point to engrave in your memories, is that any of you may be called upon to conduct them, and without prior notice. You had better know the answers."

"I think we do," remarked Moore, looking at the others.

"Those tests are comparatively trifling," pursued Commander Beckley. "It is the battle drills that are apt to give us trouble. There they will spring casualties on us."

"Casualties?"

"Yes—imaginary accidents, failures of equipment, fatalities. In battle, you know, things happen. We bump into mines. Torpedoes hit us, and shells. We overload motors and they burn up. Controls get jammed. People get hurt and drop out of the picture and somebody else has to step into their shoes and carry on. Our thermoscopes may go dead. A thousand things can go wrong. The big question is, what do we do when they do?

"Captain Allyn and his officers will work out a schedule of such casualties, neatly timed, and shoot them at us, one by one. As they do, they will make it as realistic as possible. If the primary lighting system is declared out of order, they will pull the switches. If the phones go out, they will jerk the connections in Central, and we can't touch them. If gas is reported in some compartment, they will let loose some gas in there. You can expect those casualties to come thick and fast, and you will have to know your switchboards and pipe manifolds from A to Z. It will test your versatility and coolness to the utmost."

"They ought to be able to think up some good ones," drawled Chinnery, and a few of the others laughed. The *Castor* had stripped the blades in her main auxiliary turbine only six months earlier, and she had had a serious switchboard fire during her last battle practice. Not only that, but in a recent take-off, a jet-deflector had jammed and she had spun for more than fifteen minutes about eight miles above Europa City, a gigantic pinwheel, spewing blue fire. That brought her a biting rebuke from the Patrol Force Commander.

"They will," said Beckley grimly.

There was some laughter, but there was a hint of uneasiness in some of it. Ever since the exec's crack about voice tubes, their complacency had waned. To their surprise, the voice tubes were found to be there. What else was there about the ship they did not know?

"I think that covers it," said Commander Beckley, rising. "That is, all but one feature—human casualties. It appears from this"—and he tapped the Archive Reprint—"that it was considered a rare bit of humor by our lusty ancestors to kill off the skipper early in the game, and they usually followed that promptly with the disposition of the executive officer. In this report, they killed practically all their officers in the first five minutes, and a great many of the crew with them.

"The moment an umpire declares us dead we cannot utter another word, no matter what happens. Our organization has to carry on without us. That may be a good test, but I fancy it is agonizing to watch. I recommend you put a little more attention into your drills hereafter. But above all, each of you must be prepared on an instant's notice, to succeed to the command of the ship as a whole."

"By the time we get it," observed Kingman anxiously, "she will be virtually a wreck—riddled with imaginary holes, on fire, lights out, generators dead, controls jammed, two thirds of the crew knocked out and—"

"You get it," grinned Beckley, relaxing for the first time since the captain had interrupted the meteor ball game. "Good night, boys—pleasant dreams!"

"Don't you worry, Mr. Bullard," said Tobelman, his chief turret captain, after General Quarters the next morning. "There isn't anything in this turret we can't handle, somehow."

But Bullard did worry, for he knew he was green. But he worried with a purpose. Every day of the three weeks that intervened between the exec's warning and the time set for the inspection, he plugged away at learning the ship and its intricate mechanism. By day he crawled through access and escape hatches, tracing cables and conduits; at night he pored over wiring diagrams and pipe layouts. He learned how to break down and assemble the breech mechanisms of his guns, how to train the turret by hand, and how to load in the dark. He became acquainted with the use of his standby thermoscope and practiced for an hour each day on the old Mark XIII Plotter installed in his control booth, so as to be able to maintain his own fire should his communication with the CC be cut off.

In like manner he checked his "ready" magazines and found out what he needed to know about their sprinkler systems and smothering-gas ducts. He went on beyond them and made himself familiar with the reserve magazines with their stores of TNT, ammonium nitrate, and bins of powdered aluminum. His *ammonal* he did not mix until needed, a precaution to reduce the fire hazard.

By the end of the second week he had gained a sense of confidence. In his own little department, at least, he knew his way around. And the more he worked with Tomlinson, the more he realized that back of him was a splendid bunch of boys. What he couldn't do, they would. It was in his capacity as officer of the deck that he had the most misgivings. As a watch officer, he took his regular turn in supreme command of the ship, and the more he prowled its recesses the more he was impressed by the magnitude of the task he had set himself—to learn *all* about the ship.

Every cubic yard of her vast bulk contained some machine or electrical device, the use of many of which he had but the vaguest knowledge. The *Pollux* was a very different breed of ship from the old *Asia*, relic of the Third Martian War and long overdue for the scrap heap.

On the *Asia* he had been chief engineer, and as such, knew every trick of the balky old tub, yet when he would go into the engineering compartments of the *Pollux*, he stood humble before its glittering intricacies, almost dazed by the array of strange equipment. They showed him the clustered nest of paraboloid propelling reflectors, together with their cyclotronic exciters. They traced for him the slender tubes that conveyed the pulverized Uranium 235 to the focal disintegrating points, and explained how to operate the liquid hydrogen quenching sprays. Fraser took him through the boiler rooms and sketched out for him the cycle of heat transfer, beginning with the queerly designed atomic power fire boxes, and ending with the condensers outside on the hull. Elsewhere, he examined the mercury vapor turbines and the monstrous generators they drove. In all that vast department there was but one section that struck a familiar chord. And it, he discovered, was kept locked off.

"Oh, that?" sneered Chinnery when Bullard tapped the sealed door. "A set of old oxy-hydrogen propelling motors. Standby, you know. Some dodo in the admiralty drafting room is responsible for that, I guess—supposed to be used when we are *in extremis*."

Chinnery gave a short laugh and turned away, but Bullard was persistent. He wanted to see them and check their fuel leads. At least, he had found something in this ultra-engine room he could understand at a glance.

"I forgot you came from the Crab Fleet," said Chinnery, in mock apology, "but since you ask it, you shall see those noble engines," and Chinnery beckoned to a rocketman, first-class, who stood nearby.

"Show Mr. Bullard the skeleton in our closet," said Chinnery, and departed, his spotless dungarees a mute reproach to Bullard's own grease-smeared overalls.

"I was Crab Fleet, too," grinned Benton, the rocketman, as he forced the door. "They don't think much on these Star-ships of the old liquid-fuel tubes, but you and I know what they can do. At least, you can count on 'em. These atom busters are okay when they work, but they're too temperamental to suit me. But you're the first officer I ever saw in the *Pollux* that even wanted to look at them tubes—our oars, Mr. Chinnery calls 'em."

Bullard laughed outright. The Patrol Force was a strange blend of ultramodernism and old customs, a sort of bivalence—where practical men of the old sailorman psychology used every modern gadget and hated it as he used

it; and trim, smart scientists applied archaic sea terms to
their latest triumphs.

On another day Bullard let himself into the big nose
"blister," and saw for himself the arrangement by which
the impact of stray cosmic gravel and small mines was dis-
tributed and absorbed. Beneath the false bow plate of
vanadium steel was a roomy forepeak stuffed with steel
wool, and scattered irregularly throughout were other
loosely connected plates separated by sets of spiral springs.
In general, the anti-collision compartment resembled a
titanic innerspring mattress laid across the ship's bow. A
cosmic lump striking the nose plate could not be prevented
from penetrating, but each of the inner bulkheads it pierced
gave a little, disturbing the force of the impact and slowing
down the celestial missile by a large percentage. Only a
massive body moving at relatively high velocity could retain enough velocity to crash through the last bulkhead into
the crews' quarters.

Behind the crews' quarters stood the armored bulkhead
that shielded the heart of the ship—the colossal triple-gyro
stabilizer that formed the nucleus of the egg-shaped spaceship and marked the location of the vessel's center of
gravity. It in turn was supported by a massive steel thrust
column, rising directly from the arches that held the propelling motors, and clustered around the thrust column
and in the lee of the armored stabilizer housing lay the
Central Control Room, Plot, the H.E. magazines, and the

more volatile of the chemical stores. Elsewhere in the ship were the various auxiliaries—the air-circulating fans, the renewers, and the garbage converters, and all the rest of the multitudinous motors for every purpose.

Bullard was exhausted; mentally and physically, by the time he had completed the comprehensive survey, but he felt better for having done it. In his journeys he had missed nothing, taking in storerooms as well as machinery spaces, viewing the planetary bombing racks recessed in the landing skids, and the selenium helio-generators on the upper halves of the hull. There were many details he knew he had not fully grasped, but the main thing was he had regained his customary self-confidence. He no longer felt himself a stranger on the ship.

The others had not been idle, either. Intensive drills had been held daily in all departments, and as nearly as was humanly possible, every conceivable contingency had been foreseen and provided for.

"If those Castor Beans have thought up just half the stunts I have," observed Kingman, at the end of a strenuous day's preparations, "this inspection is going to be a honey. But what the hell! My conscience don't hurt. If there is anything unprovided for, it's the fault of my lack of imagination—nothing else."

"Yeah," grunted Chinnery. Chinnery had become a trifle touchy over the coming ordeal. The exec had made him clear out the old battery room and reinstall his storage batteries.

"They say," chimed in another, "that Freddy McCaskey

is going to make Moore set the ship down on top that spiny ridge at the north end of Io, with two of his underjets out of commission. To make it tough they are going to put an egg on the chart rack. If it falls off and busts when he hits, the mark will be a swab-o."

"Scuttlebutt, you dope," commented Fraser, "nobody knows what they'll spring on us. But, personally, my money is on the old *Pollux*. All that's worrying me is—"

And on and on it went. Speculation was rife in every nook and cranny of the powerful sky cruiser. The lowest rating on board tossed feverishly in his hammock throughout the rest period called "night," trying to imagine what crazy orders might be given him, and what he would do about it when he got them. The Polliwogs were agreed on one thing, though. Come what might, the only visible reaction any umpire would get, would be a cheery "Aye, aye, sir." Deadpan compliance was the password. They swore that under no circumstances would any of them display surprise or dismay.

Came the momentous day. Clean as a shower-washed sky and burnished and polished until she shone with almost painful brilliance, the *Pollux* lay proudly in her launching cradle at Ursapolis Yard. To the shrilling of pipes, another vestige of age-old tradition, the spry little admiral clambered aboard, his staff at his heels, for the first stage of the inspection.

His trip through the spotless compartments was swift. Although few details of the interior could have escaped his darting glances, he took no notes, nor did he pause at any place to make comment. It was not until he had completed his tour that he broke his silence.

"She *looks* good," he said cryptically to Captain Dongan. Whereupon he trotted off to his quarters in the yard for his lunch, sending back word that he would return in two hours for the remainder of the exercises.

"Cinch!" muttered someone, but the captain wheeled and scowled at him. To the captain's mind, the admiral's serene disregard for the snowy whiteness of the paint work was significant. Plainly, the old man's interest was centered elsewhere, and that could only be on the practical tests. It was not that the captain was especially dubious as to the outcome—he merely wondered. After all, as he had told Beckley, they had never really been inspected before.

Hardly had the admiral left than the Castor Beans began pouring aboard. The enlisted men came first, swarming down the dock and waving their notebooks.

"Hi-ya, Pollutes!" they yelled. "Boy, if you only knew!" Grinning Polliwogs let them aboard and led them off into the recesses of the ship, hoping, while their umpires were in a boastful mood, to worm some of their secrets from them in advance. A little later Captain Allyn and his officers came, and later, at the appointed hour, the admiral.

"Ahem," announced the admiral, his words very crisp, for all his high-pitched, thin voice. "The *Pollux* will lay a course past Jupiter to the small, innermost satellite, now in opposition. She will land on it, then take off and return to base. During the problem, she shall not communicate with nor receive assistance from the outside. At various times, as we go, we shall hold drills, introducing various casualties. It must be understood that these artificial casualties are to be treated in every respect as if they were real, and if the ship departs in any manner from such treatment, the score for the tests shall be zero."

Captain Dongan acknowledged the admiral's instructions with a nod.

"And let me add," went on the admiral, "that should there, by chance, occur any real accident or casualty, it shall be treated as part of the problem. Are you ready, gentlemen?"

Carlson, the baby of the mess, drew the take-off, and despite a rather obvious self-consciousness, managed it well. The ship drew upward cleanly and smoothly, and gradually curved like a soaring eagle toward the great rose disk of the System's primary. Carlson drew a perfunctory, "Well done," from the chief umpire, and withdrew, mopping his brow in relief. It was Kingman who succeeded him.

"Fire in the paint locker!" was what Kingman had to deal with—the commonest and most obvious of fire drills. People ran to their stations in jig time and were duly checked off. Their performance was faultless, their apparatus was in perfect condition, the most carping critic could find nothing to complain of. A great load rolled off the exec's troubled mind. Fire in the paint locker, indeed! If they kept on springing chestnuts like that, this expedition would be a picnic.

"And think of all the useless work he put us to," crabbed Chinnery into Fraser's ear.

It fell to Fraser's lot to conduct the Abandon Ship Drill. The Polliwogs were tense as televox repeaters throughout the ship chanted the call to the boats. Number 3, on the starboard side, was a balky slut. Five times out of six her tube would not fire unless preheated with a blowtorch. It was a mystery why, for they had successively put in four spares and still Number 3 performed in the same erratic manner. But today she took off like a startled dove at the first touch of the coxswain's button. Pure luck that was, for there was not a chance to use the torch with watchful umpires writing down all they saw.

The Castor Beans pawed through the returned boats, looking for error, but their search was unsuccessful. Boat boxes were correct, down to the first aid kit, as was the power installation and the handling. Fraser drew another four-o and was excused.

Bullard was called up and there was a long lull. They were inside Ganymede's orbit before the umpires raised the alarm of collision. That, too, was expeditiously dealt with, although a penalty of one tenth of a point was assessed because a third-rate carpenter's mate in his haste entered the air-exhausted compartment before putting his vacuum helmet on. When Bullard heard that that was all that was wrong, he drew a deep breath and relaxed. It was annoying to have sullied the ship's hitherto perfect score with a penalty, but it could well have been worse.

Moore drew the "Search and Rescue Party" and while the ship hove to above Mount Sarpedon in Equatorial Europa, descended into that noisome crater and found and brought back the dummy which an aid of the admiral had planted there some days before. It was a triumph for the *Pollux*, for the dummy was lying smack in the midst of the dreaded Halogen Geysers. Raw fluorine is hard on standard equipment, but the *Pollux's* rescue boat carried what it took. Aside from a mild gassing of two members of the boat's crew, there were no mishaps.

The admiral was standing on the boat deck when Moore came back. He stared at the remnants of the corroded dummy and at the pitted helmets and reeking suits of the rescue party. A Castorian umpire stepped out of the boat and reported the two cases of gassing.

"Too nice work to spoil with a penalty," decreed the old man. "Chalk up a four-o for Lieutenant Moore."

That night the mess was jubilant. They were two thirds the way through the inspection and hadn't slipped yet— except for that fractional point against Bullard. No one reproached him for that, for it was not that kind of a mess, but Bullard was none too happy. Had there been other penalties, he would not have minded, but this one stood glaring in its loneliness.

"We're better than you thought, eh?" said Beckley, slapping Abel Warlock, exec of the *Castor*, on the back.

"You're not out of the woods, yet," was Warlock's dry

rejoinder, and he threw a wink to Pete Roswell. "Tomorrow's another day."

Io was under the stern and drawing aft when General Quarters was sounded. Men tumbled to their battle stations and manned their weapons. Bullard crawled into his control booth and strapped on his headphone. "Ready," he reported, after an instantaneous checkup of his turret crew. Every man was at his post, poised and ready.

It was a tableau that was repeated all over the ship. Captain Dongan was at Control, the exec in Plot, and down the line each was where he should be. And beside each was the inevitable umpire with his ticking watch and his telltale notebook. Now was the hour. Here is where the fun began. Were the Polliwogs fair-weather sailors or what?

"Start watches," signaled the chief umpire, and the problem was begun.

At four and a half seconds, Bullard let go his first salvo. Swiftly his men threw in the second load.

The machinery-packed turret was uncomfortably full of men, what with the doubling up due to the presence of the umpires. These latter were dancing about, trying to keep out of the way while at the same time recording the fire-control data as it came in over the visuals, or otherwise making notes of the efforts of the *Pollux* men. In the booth with Bullard was Heine Bissel, the turret officer of the *Castor*, keeping one eye on what Bullard was doing and the other peeking at the list of casualties in his hand. Bullard envied the umpires their freedom of movement, for unlike the men at battle stations, there was no necessity for the umpires to dress themselves in spacesuits. In battle, of course, suits were donned before its commencement. A chance hit, penetrating an outer bulkhead, might at any instant cause a compartment to lose its air.

Bullard's second salvo went, but coincidentally with it the lights flickered, dimmed a moment, then blazed up again. Somewhere below something had gone wrong with the primary lighting circuit and there had been a shift made to another.

"Your ammunition hoist motors are inoperative," announced Bissel, looking at his list.

"Hoist by hand!" ordered Bullard, almost in the same breath. He attempted to report the casualty to CC, but the phone was dead on his ears. He snatched its jack from the outlet and plugged in on No. 2 circuit. It was dead.

His men managed to get the guns fired a third time. It was a full three seconds late, due to the delay occasioned by having to serve the guns by hand, but under the circumstances, in good time. Bullard saw them ram the fourth set of projectiles home. His eyes caught the racing words on the telescribe above his head, "Transverse hit penetrated both CC and Plot—captain and executive dead—control now in sub-CC—Chinnery commanding."

"Your lights have gone out," remarked Bissel, with a triumphant gleam in his eye, reaching for the cutout switch overhead. The lights *were* out.

Bullard kicked out with his left foot and found the emergency battery switch. Again there was light, this time from the turret's own batteries, independent of any general ship's circuit. Tobelman shot the propellant into the breech of the last gun and closed the firing key. There was no recoil. He jerked the lanyard and fired the guns by percussion. At that moment an umpire rose from behind the loading tray and fired a pan of flashlight powder. There was an instant's brilliance, blinding in its intensity. Then all was black.

"Your battery has short-circuited," came the calm voice of Bissel through the murk. There was suppressed amusement in it, and Bullard suspected this last casualty was an improvised one. But it did not matter. Bissel had kicked the turret switch open again, and that made it official.

"Loaded in dark, sir!" called Tobelman. "Ready!"

"Fire!" Bullard was proud of his gang.

"Enemy shell just entered and wiped out turret crew," whispered Bissel. There was silence outside the booth as the men desisted from their efforts in the dark. Each had been told the same thing by his own umpire. Bissel snapped on a portable flash long enough to jot down the time of the massacre.

"Am I dead, too?" inquired Bullard.

"Oh, no. You're all right. Your turret is all shot, that's all."

Bullard dived out of the escape hatch. If all his men were dead, there was nothing to be gained by sitting in the darkened control booth waiting for the end. His duty was elsewhere.

The elevator was stuck between decks, probably another casualty. Bullard, trailed by the panting Bissel, flung himself down the ladder and dropped through the armored hatchway into CC. It was empty, except for a couple of lounging umpires, comparing notes. Bullard cast an anxious eye at the settings on the main control board, but with it saw that the master switch at the top of it was open. Control, of course, had been shifted elsewhere. The positions of the controls here, regardless of how they were set, were meaningless.

He dashed down the passage toward sub-CC, a little cubbyhole abaft Plot, not wasting a second in a futile stop at the Plotting Room. What he had seen in CC would doubtless be repeated there. As he passed the door of the wardroom he caught a glimpse of the officers crowded in there, and what he saw made him pause a moment and take a closer look. Peering through the glassite panel he was astonished to see most of the officers of the *Pollux* in there, either out of their spacesuits or in the act of taking them off. Chinnery, whom he thought in temporary command, was one of them.

"The corpses," grinned Bissel. "They are where they won't interfere and they may as well be comfortable."

But from the indications, Captain Dongan was anything but comfortable. He was pacing the deck impatiently, grave concern in every line of his rugged face. Beckley looked scarcely less uneasy.

Bullard hurried on. He had seen every one of his brother officers in there except Fraser. Could it be that he and Fraser were the only survivors? He jerked the door of sub-CC open. The place was a madhouse, five men stationed at voice tubes yelling to five other men in some other place —and each of the five communications was a different one.

"Thought you were dead," exclaimed Fraser, seeing Bullard come bursting in. "Everything has gone to pot and communications are terrible, but if you are looking for a job, jump down into the engine room and make a check—"

"Apoplexy!" screamed an excited umpire, pointing at Fraser. "You! You're dead."

Fraser choked his words in the middle, stamped a foot in disgust, and jerked off his helmet. He turned in the doorway and looked as if he was about to say something; then, as if thinking better of it, stalked off toward the wardroom to join the rest of the "dead."

Bullard suddenly realized that he was left in command on the ship, but he had not the faintest idea of her running condition, beyond knowing from her heave that she was still accelerating full power. Until he could learn what had happened and what was left in operating condition, he could give no intelligent orders. Then it was that he saw the admiral, Captain Allyn, Commander Warlock and others watching him intently, through the broad deadlight let into the bulkhead between Plot and the sub-CC. So *he* was to be the goat of this inspection! A sorry trick. He, the next most junior officer on the ship and the latest to join her, put to this severe test! It angered him, but the thought as suddenly struck him that the test was also one of the *Pollux*. As long as any man of her complement remained alive, he must carry on. These foxy umpires must be shown that the *Pollux* was prepared, and well prepared. The three tedious weeks of intensive drills and the unceasing labors of the captain and his exec in teaching their men must not be in vain. If the ship still could be handled, he would handle it!

"Silence!" he roared. The weary talkers at the voice tubes looked at him and blinked. He flung a finger at the first one. "Report!"

One by one, the five told the story, staccato words coming fast. As the details appeared, Bullard was aghast at the task set for him. The torpedo room, like the turret, was out of commission, its crew wiped out. There was a fire raging in the chemical stores locker. The great mercury boilers were shut down, their superheaters riddled and leaking, and as a result, all auxiliary power was off. There was only the weak and inadequate current flowing in from the helio units, sufficient only to maintain the standing lights. All means of communication were gone except voice tubes. And to cap the climax, the main jets were said to be jammed—full speed ahead. And ahead, perilously close, lay Jupiter—Jupiter the colossal, the huge, the devouring magnet. Drill or no drill, something must be done, and that very soon.

As Bullard sprang into action, he wondered how long

the farce of imaginary disabilities would be kept up. Yet until the war game was called off he could touch none of the umpire-guarded valves or switches. He had to work with the disorganized residuum of the mighty ship's power. A new note of danger began to hum, warning him that whatever he was to do could no longer be postponed. Since the automatic controllers on the uranium feed lines were not operating, the acceleration was slowly picking up—when he wanted none at all he was getting more—and there was no way of cutting it off except manually.

He raised the tube room and found to his immense satisfaction that it was Benton, the rocketman, who was in charge there. Benton assured him there was no way to shut off the uranium flow other than by using the forbidden electrically controlled valves.

"Get pipe cutters, then, or Stilsons, and *break* the lines!"

"Aye, aye, sir."

Bullard knew that Benton knew that the uranium would continue to dribble out, wasting into the wake, but unless it was fed to the exact focus of the disintegrating inferno, it could not flare into the tremendous energy of exploding atoms. Once the supply was cut off, the quenching sprays would make short work of the bits still at the focal points.

An insistent call kept coming from the chemical locker, where the fire was supposed to be. The Polliwog there complained that the umpire would declare him burnt to a crisp unless some action was taken to subdue the fire. For a moment, Bullard hesitated. Actually, there was nothing inflammable in the chemical locker—except the fireworks flare the umpires had set themselves to add realism to their act —and consequently the compartment was not fitted with fire-fighting devices.

"Evacuate the storeroom," ordered Bullard. "Gather up all the *Pollux* men near you and transfer everything in it to the reserve magazine inboard of you."

"Aye, aye, sir," came the voice, relieved from his dilemma of having either to abandon his post or be roasted alive.

Bullard felt the lagging of the vessel as the acceleration ceased and knew that Benton had succeeded in breaking the atomic feed lines. It was a pity to have to waste power in that fashion, but it was unthinkable to continue longer on a power dive into Jupiter. The jet-deflectors were locked rigidly fore and aft and there could be no turning with those jets. He got Benton to the voice tube once more.

"What's wrong with the old rudder flaps over the liquid tube jets?"

"Not a damn thing, sir."

"Then warm up your tubes and let's get going—"

"Aye, aye, sir."

"And, Benton, when they've started spewing, flip 'er halfway around and shoot ninety degrees from the present course. You'll have to do that by local control—there is none for those old tubes in this substation."

"Aye, aye, sir."

Bullard felt better. He was devoutly thankful they had spared Benton for him. Benton was a man of parts. Shortly they would have this wildly careering warship under some degree of control. Then Bullard could proceed with some of the badly needed minor corrections. One thing that was a source of great annoyance was the all-pervading noise, much augmented by the shouts of his voice tube talkers. He decided to abandon the use of the archaic tubes and, instead, employ the etherphones in their space helmets. It meant setting up a manifold party line, for the helmet phones were not selective and if everyone should start talking at once the result would be babel.

"Tell all hands," he directed the group of talkers in sub-CC, "to close their face plates and tune in on the etherphone. No one is to speak except in answer to me or to report an exceptional emergency."

The word was passed. Bullard, to check the efficiency of this means of communications, called the various parts of the ship in succession to receive their reports. There were a gratifying number of men still alive and at their posts, despite the wholesale slaughter of the officers. It was not until he checked on the chemical locker fire that he heard anything to disturb him unduly. All was going well until the wild laughter and silly words of the man in charge of the reserve magazine rang in his helmet. Bullard snapped back harsh questions, and for answer got only maudlin ravings, interspersed with outbursts of giggling. The man was drunk—or something.

Bullard glanced sharply in the direction of the admiral and the knot of inspecting officers watching him from Plot. They, too, showed some signs of glee, several of them grinning vacuously. Pete Roswell was executing an awkward burlesque of the *quilliota*, a dance often seen in the cabarets of Ursapolis. A sudden anger surged within Bullard. Had they turned the inspection into an outright farce? A bad joke at his expense? As he stared indignantly at the group in Plot, he was further outraged to see Abel Warlock waggishly begin ripping the meter leads from their terminals. And—of all things—the admiral himself, was capering about madly, an absurd elfin smirk spread across his usually ultradignified features.

Again Bullard sharply challenged his man in the magazine. This time the voice that came back was more sober— almost penitent.

"Sorry, sir—had a crazy dream, I guess. But it was awfully funny, sir." As he talked his voice grew even more sober and more contrite. "And sir, I ought to tell you—the umpires have passed out. They're lying around all over the place—"

A funny dream! Umpires dropping unconscious! Bullard lost not a second. With a bound he left sub-CC, headed for the trunk leading down to the magazines.

He fought his way through the smoke of the flares, passed through the half-emptied chemical locker and into the reserve magazine. Dimly he saw his magazine keeper bending over several limp forms on the deck. Bullard paused to examine the smoke bomb but was convinced that it was not the cause of what was wrong. It was a standard product— a mixture of luciferin with a little strontium salts, giving at once a ruddy flame and considerable quantities of smoke, yet without much heat. Its fumes were neither intoxicating nor hypnotic.

He saw that much of the miscellaneous assortment of chemicals that had been stowed in the locker were now standing about the floor of the magazine, but all of them were ordinary substances and not regarded as hazardous. There were barrels of various salts and carboys of acids, but none of those were broken. On top of the pile stood three roundish flat crystal flasks of nearly black liquid. He recognized them as containers of an iodine solution—also harmless.

Before going to assist his man in reviving the stricken umpires, Bullard opened his face plate by a tiny crack and took a cautious sniff. Ah! That sickly sweetish odor was strangely familiar. And as a queer ringing in his ears began he snapped his helmet shut and fumbled for his oxygen valve. He kept a firm grip on his consciousness; he knew that in a second his momentary giddiness would pass, for the whiff he had had was nothing more noxious than nitrous oxide. But where was the N_2O coming from, and how much of it was there?

He sprang to the bin holding the ammonium nitrate. To the eye it was normal, yet his reason told him it must be the source of these fumes. He moved closer to it and was suddenly aware of a warm spot between his shoulder blades. It was as if he had stepped in front of a firebox door. He wheeled to see the source of the heat, and saw—only the three flasks of iodine, and behind and beyond them the lazy smoke of the dying flare.

His bewilderment left him with a rush. The situation was transparently clear. The iodine flasks, shaped as they were, were acting as focusing lenses for the infrared rays from the smudge bomb, concentrating its weak heat until it was plainly perceptible. Under the influence of that mild heating, the ammonium nitrate had begun to break down and give off the nitrous oxide fumes. Now he understood the lunatic behavior of the magazine man before he shut his face plate, and why the umpires were lying unconscious about the place. He flung himself at the iodine lenses and dashed them to the deck. Then he leaped to the atmospheric control valves on the bulkhead and stepped up the amount of oxygen entering the compartment. He called to Benton in the tube room and ordered him to hook up the storage batteries hitherto held in reserve, and put power on the blowers. He must clear the magazine of the "laughing gas."

"Laughing gas!" The antics of the inspecting officers! Now it began to make sense. He shot a glance at the open voice tubes and knew in that instant what had occurred. And knowing it, he shuddered to think of what might be going on above. The nitrous oxide, being heavier than air, was naturally flowing through the open tubes toward the control room and the other compartments clustered about the ship's center of gravity. All those unhelmeted officers, those of the *Pollux*, as well as the Castorian inspectors, would be tipsy at the very least. Perhaps by now they were dropping unconscious. Bullard snapped shut the gastight voice tube covers and shouted warnings into his helmet phone to his other men throughout the ship.

"Too late," came back Benton's report. "They're acting like crazy men—but how was I to know? I couldn't smell and I thought it was all part of the game. Only now—"

"Only now what?" snapped Bullard, his heart sinking.

"Well," reported Benton, hesitant to quote so august a personage as the Commander of the Jovian Patrol Force when the latter was in an uninhibited mood, "the admiral came dancing in and slapped our captain on the back and said, 'Let's make it a good party,' and Captain Mike said, 'Sure! You've overlooked a lot of bets—' "

Bullard groaned. The stuff must have seeped into the wardroom, too.

"Then they all laughed like hell and began busting things."

Bullard listened dully as Benton recited the list of outrages. Cables had been torn out bodily, others crazily connected and short-circuited; controls were smashed and the needles on gauges twisted to weird angles; in short, they had raised hell generally. The hilarious victims of the gas had made every one—and more—of the invented casualties a grim reality. Now the ship *was* out of control.

"Keep shooting the oxygen to them," yelled Bullard. "I'm on my way up."

Benton had not overstated the case. The CC, Plot, subplot and the engine spaces suggested the wake of a terrestrial typhoon. The decks were cluttered with controller handles, broken dials and tattered paper. They had even torn up the astragational tables and the log. From the bulkheads dangled the stray ends of leads and bashed-in indicators.

The place was an unholy mess. And all about sat the droop-
ing officers who had done it, too groggy by then to do more,
but still staring about with imbecilic expressions.

There was no use crying over spilt milk. Outside was the
threat of Jupiter, more ominous than before, and Bullard
was reminded of it as he felt the thrust when the six old-
fashioned liquid-fuel tubes fired their first blast. Good old
Benton! Despite the madhouse raging about him, he had
persevered with the task assigned and had got them to firing. The ship lurched in reaction and with the lurch many
of the dizzy observers were flung to the nearest bulkhead.
The busy hospital corpsmen, darting among them with their
first aid kits, had a fresh problem to cope with. Some of
their patients were doubly unconscious.

Bullard might have been more concerned with the comfort of his stricken seniors, but hard on the heels of the
success in getting the tubes to blasting came a new casualty,
and an utterly unforeseen one. A strange throb shivered
through the ship and she began to tilt unaccountably, and
with it came a violent sidewise oscillation that made the
skin crawl. A still conscious umpire huddled in a corner
gave way frankly to his nausea; dangling wreckage battered
against the bulkheads while the rubbish strewn about the
decks shifted back and forward like the tides of the sea.
The din and clatter of it was unbearable.

Above it all rose the shrilling whine of runaway motors.
As the wild and sickening oscillations increased in ampli-
tude it became painfully apparent that something was hap-
pening to the massive whirling gyros at the heart of the

vessel. Bullard fought his way toward them, clinging to such projections his hands could reach and dodging the missiles of débris flung about by the bucking ship. In time, he reached the armored door of the gyro housing and by then he had gained an inkling of what had gone wrong, but the remedy for it was not so obvious.

In their drunken orgy of devastation, the umpires had broken the leads feeding the motor field coils, and the gyros were running away—but at unequal rates, probably due to the inequalities of their own bearing frictions. Bullard knew, of course, that he could cut off the armature current, but if he did that the acceleration would shortly be reversed. Should the gyros be slowed rapidly, their rotational momentum would be transferred to the ship and force it into a dizzy whirling, a condition the crew could not endure. Bullard had scant hope of being able to restore the field current. Finding the breaks among the tangle of wreckage would take hours, whereas he had only minutes available, and not many of those.

"Send me a man and plenty of stray cable," he called to Benton, "and I want juice up to the gyro housing from the batteries."

Bullard was looking at the steel columns that held the bearings of the gyro axles—six of them, in pairs, each pair at right angles to the others. What he could not do by electrical resistance he would do by friction. If he could regulate the bearing thrust, he could keep the speed of the gyros under control. It had looked hopeless to him at first, for there was no way to insert the huge jacks they had on board, but he had thought of a way that was at least worth a trial.

"Throw the end of that cable around there," he directed, "and make a coil—a helix—around that bearing column. I intend to magnetize it."

The man—one of Fraser's—did as he was told, but the unbelief in his face was easy to read. What difference did it make whether the thrust columns were magnetic or not?

"That's well!" shouted Bullard, when the last of the six had been wound. Then he ordered current—a weak current, but under his instant control by means of the rheostats he had had inserted in the lines. It had been a tough job, getting that far, for all the while they had been flung this way and that as the whirling masses of metal fought to take charge of the battered cruiser. But Bullard and his helpers had hung on, and now was to come the test.

He was rewarded, after a little, by the halting of the steadily rising crescendo of the motor wail. At least he had stopped the acceleration. Now all he had to do was bring the three into harmony.

"You've got the idea," he said to the principal electrician who had been helping him. "Keep monkeying with them until they are all together. The bearings will get hot, but we can't help that. Flood 'em with oil, and if that doesn't do it, send down for some liquid air. Whatever you do, don't let 'em freeze, or we'll be flung clear out of the System."

"Aye, aye, sir," said the man, "but how did we do it?"

"Magnetostriction," Bullard explained, as he prepared to slip from the compartment. "A *little* magnetism makes steel expand, that's all. If your bearings get too tight, give 'em either more juice or less, and you'll shorten those columns."

Bullard slid out of the housing and picked his way aft. He wondered where they were by now and whether they would win their fight with Jupiter. He could feel the surge of the ship as the six flaming tubes drove it, and knew from his sense of weight that they were pulling out—but how fast?

Benton looked worried. His tubes were behaving wonderfully, but they lacked power for the job imposed. The *Pollux* was checked in her fall, and that was all. She needed more kick to escape, and Benton did not dare apply it. Bullard came and looked.

"Can't be helped," he muttered, "give 'er the works."

"They'll melt," warned Benton.

"Let 'em," said the youthful acting captain, with grim finality. "We can't be any worse off."

Benton shrugged, and began the doubling of his fuel lines. Others of his men scurried off to storerooms and presently came back, lugging spare injectors. Those, after a few minutes of frenzied work, were coupled with improvised superchargers and inserted into the new fuel into the laboring tubes, the *Pollux*'s wake bloomed from a mere meteoric streak of ruddy fire to the whitely dazzling fan of a Grade A comet. Her determined masters piled gravity after gravity onto her acceleration, building her up until her men could stand no more, despite copious injections of *gravonol.* Harried hospital corpsmen had been pulled off their work of salvaging the unhappy "dead" and the Castorian umpires long enough to administer those precautionary shots.

Presently a sobered and grave-faced chief umpire—Captain Allyn of the *Castor*—staggered into the tube room, supported by two of his junior officers. All of them looked the worse for wear, bruised and cut as they were and only partially bandaged, but at least they had managed to get onto their feet. Like everyone else, while still woozy from the effects of the gas they had been badly flung about during the bout with the rebellious gyros.

"The admiral says," Captain Allyn announced, "that all imposed casualties are rescinded. Cease present exercises and return to base."

"Like hell he does!" snorted Bullard, flaring with resentment. "You tell the admiral he lacks authority to rescind the casualties *I'm* contending with. You can tell him that I'll get out of here how, when, and if I can; and that it will be time enough after that to talk about ceasing something and returning somewhere. In the meantime, kindly get out of that man's way. He has real work to do."

Captain Allyn opened his one good eye in blank astonishment, but he stepped to one side and let the burdened tube man pass with his armful of fresh spare parts. The skipper of the *Castor* looked from the angry young man in his soiled and torn uniform to the chaotic tube room about him, and then back again. He had not realized what a pass things had come to. There were no instruments of any kind in working order, either astragational or engineering. These sweating, strained-looking men could only guess at the pressures, voltages, amperages and the rest that they were dealing with. Now, if ever, a man had to have the *feel* of a ship—and this one had an awkward feel, a terrible feel. It was the sickening feeling of doom.

"There goes the first one," remarked Benton calmly, as the ship shuddered and gave a little jump. They felt, rather than heard, the increased roar outside, and a white-faced man sitting astride the smoking supercharger in number 4 tube feedline frantically fought to close the valve beneath him. The first of the overtaxed liners had reached the ultimate temperature—had been volatilized and sneezed out into Jupiter's face. Benton's voice was quiet and the lines about his chin unquavering, but there was anxiety in his eyes.

"Hang on," said Bullard. "We can't ease off now. The others may be tougher. We're going uphill now—if they'll only last half an hour we'll be over the hump."

Captain Allyn and his two aids discreetly withdrew to a corner of the tube room. He was too competent an officer to meddle, now that he had some understanding of the situation, and he could see that this dirty-faced lad knew what he was about. He contented himself with putting a few additional entries into his already crowded notebook.

It was nearly twenty minutes before the next tube collapsed to be hurled into the wake as a cloud of vividly incandescent vapor. That was number 3, and five minutes later went number 1—and almost simultaneously with it, number 6. But the other two held out until they reached the crest, and beyond. The critical point was passed, judging by the feel of things, and the order was on Bullard's lips to cut the blasts by twenty percent when one of the remaining tubes let go, too. That left but one, all the motive power the ship had, and that woefully inadequate, but at least they were moving outward into the clean, dark depths of the ether. Bullard cut its output hastily until it was down to normal, wondering hopefully as he did whether they were out of the woods yet.

He left the oppressively hot tube room to Benton and his gang and went out into the disordered ship in search of an altiscope. For minutes he struggled through cluttered passages and choked trunks, looking into the now deserted turrets and other fire-control stations for an unsmashed instrument that bore. It was in the topsy-turvy wreckage of the torpedo room he found one, and it was with a sense of almost dread that he put his eyes to it and took a squint at Jupiter. Then his heart leaped with joy and relief, for the great rose disk took up only part of the telescopic field and as he hastily read the graduations along the cross hairs he saw they were out of the worst of its gravitational field. In fact, they must be not far from the orbit of the small satellite that was their destination.

Bullard whirled the altiscope until he brought the tiny iron body into his field of vision, and the moment he sighted it he began barking orders to his men back in the tube room. They must turn now, and with their single good tube and the five frayed and oversized ones buck their own forward momentum. The problem had shifted from the desperate need for acceleration to the necessity of checking their flight. To conform to the terms of the admiral's order, they must land on that barren lump of iron.

Somehow they did it. It may have been four hours later, or six, for time had ceased to have meaning, when a haggard and very dirty young lieutenant and the exhausted remnants of his crew staggered out onto the black plain of Jupiter's inmost satellite. They wasted but a moment in staring up at the huge hulk that had brought them there. Outwardly, she was the sleek, powerful cruiser that she had been the day before, however disarranged she might be inside, but they were not concerned with her general appearance. They had come to inspect the damage done to her afterhull by the disintegration of the tube liners. Was it irreparable? And what sort of terrain lay beneath the now helpless Pride of the Skies?

For Lieutenant Bullard was not content with merely having escaped the grip of Jupiter. As he understood it, he was in temporary command of the *Pollux*; and of the tactical problem assigned only the first leg had been completed. He must get off this rock next and take her back to Ursapolis and set her down in her launching cradle in the yard. Benton shook his head gloomily. There were no more rabbits in the hat. To sit down on Callisto they would need not one tube but three, and at that, the maneuver was sure to be jerky and full of risk.

It was while these two were in their huddle, talking over ways and means that the admiral and Captain Dongan found them. Allyn had roused them and told them where to look.

"Well done, Bullard," said Captain Mike. "The admiral has promised you a special commendation. Tell me now the exact condition of the ship and I will relieve you. The first thing the admiral wants is a jury-rigged radio so we can have tugs come out. As soon as that is done you may go and rest. I'll take charge now."

"No, sir," protested Bullard hotly. "I *demand* the right to carry on. They have put us into this mess as a test. Well —the test is not over yet. According to the rules, if we call for help, we lose. We can't—"

"We have not lost," said Captain Mike quietly. "The problem has been canceled. Unforeseen developments—"

"Yes!" cried Bullard, his voice almost a scream, he was so outraged at the implications, "that's just it—unforeseen developments, and the *Pollux* couldn't take it! That is what the sky fleet will be saying and laughing at us in every mess from Pluto to Mercury. If we let 'em call this thing off now, we're all washed up and done as far as being the best ship in the whole—"

Bullard was a bit hysterical and quite unaware of his seeming insubordination. He had been through a lot and his nerves were frayed and jumpy, but for hours now he had concentrated on this dilemma and he was in no mood to be shoved to one side. It was up to him to find a way out —he *must* find a way out, one way or another. Any other

solution would be to let the *Pollux* down, an admitted failure, and that was unthinkable. After all, what was this
unforeseen development that had wrecked them? Nitrous
oxide! So what? That was a legitimate hazard. It could
have been generated under other and more normal conditions and would have had to have been dealt with. To call
off this test now would be simply to take refuge behind an
alibi, and a weak one at that. Bullard was the one the umpires had chosen for the guinea pig and he couldn't quit. As
he saw it, not only was the reputation of the ship at stake,
but his own personal honor.

Hot words poured from him, reckless words—mutinous-
sounding, but Captain Mike listened gravely. He looked at
this lieutenant of his thoughtfully.

"I like your spirit, Bullard, but that is beside the point.
There is no way out now. It is too late. As for your reputation, have no fear—"

"Oh, that's not it, sir—" Bullard was on the verge of
tears.

"Let the boy have his way," interposed the admiral. "His
stand is the correct one. Personally, I think we're wasting
time, but I won't have it said that I denied justice to any
man. If he thinks he can pull out of here, let him try it. I
will allot you twenty-four more hours to carry on the problem, Bullard, and during that time you will have no interference. Good luck!"

If Bullard's tears had been close to the surface from rage
and anger, the reason a few dribbled down his cheeks now
was a different one. His first emotion was jubilation. But in

a moment that gave way to a sense of awe as the full implication of what he had assumed made itself apparent to him.
He realized that in insisting on carrying this problem to its
conclusion he had put both himself and the *Pollux* on the
spot. Before, they had at least an out—a plausible and an
officially acceptable alibi. If he failed now, the ship failed
with him. Remorse smote him. Had his vanity led him to
compromise the name of this ship he had become so attached to? It was a sobering thought. Now he knew, as he
never had before, that he must succeed. Not until the *Pollux* was snugged down in the yard could he rid himself of
the responsibility.

That thought was all the bracer he needed. As by a miracle, his fatigue dropped away from him, and by a few
terse words he managed to convey to Benton and his helpers
something of the same fiery spirit that animated him. To a
man, they knew that excuses would have no value—they
must deliver.

It was an interested group of spectators who thronged
about the grounded cruiser. By common consent the rules
had been relaxed to the extent that the "dead" could look
on and converse, provided only they did not interfere. From
the deceased Polliwogs came words of cheer—the whole
crew was rooting for them, while now and then a Castor
Bean would relieve himself of some wisecrack at the expense of the toiling repair men. The admiral, for all his
magnanimity, was fretful and impatient. He had a dinner
date with the Governor of Callisto for the following evening and it annoyed him to think he might not be there.

The Castorians, too, were anxious to get back to the yard. They yearned to get aboard their own vessel, for in the last few hours they had learned there was much to do to that fine ship. Her inspection—by the Polliwogs—was set for the following week.

Bullard doggedly disregarded them all. He had opened a cargo hatch along the keelson and from the nether hold his men had dragged five huge cylinders. Using heavy tackles, they ranged them alongside the *Pollux* in the wan sunlight of the Jovian System. Farther aft, heavy tripods had been set up and diamond-pointed drills were biting into the native iron of the little satellite. Other men were high up on the sternpost, driving portable reamers into the ragged tunnels of the tube housings. Chinnery and Roswell, chief engineers respectively of the *Pollux* and *Castor*, stood by, watching.

Chinnery evinced no joy at seeing this young officer from the gunnery department making bold with his spare stores, nor did he take pains to conceal his contempt for this latest effort.

"Spare bushings for the old-style tubes," he explained to Roswell. "I forgot I had a set. But they won't do him any good. They're oversized. We carry 'em because they are too big forgings to pick up anywhere, but it takes a well-equipped yard to put 'em in—they have to be pressed in, you know, to a tight fit."

Roswell nodded. As a rival, he was quite willing to see the job miscarry. Up until then, the *Pollux* had parried every one of his devastating casualties. He was hoping they would muff this real one.

But Bullard neither knew nor cared what they were saying. He and Benton were on top one of the huge tubes, manipulating a gigantic pair of calipers. They already knew they were oversize, and their plans for pressing them in were at that very moment in the process of execution. Astern of the ship a group of holes had been drilled into the iron, and now the men had substituted fat taps for the drills. Those who had originally brought the tubes out of the storeroom were back within the ship, rousing out hundreds of fathoms of high tensile chain—carried for the rare emergency of a heavy tow.

The men up in the tubes reported their job completed, but Bullard frowned when he read the finished diameter. It was too little. He wished ardently for a giant lathe so he could take a cut off the massive tubes. But there was no such lathe nearer than Ursapolis. He would have to reduce the outer diameter of the bushings some other way.

He bled air from the ship through outlets on its shady side, and collected the liquefied gas in buckets and doused the tubes with the cold liquid air, but even when they had shrunk to their minimum size, they were still too large. It was a disappointment, for he had little time to spare for the actual work ahead and none at all for experimentation. The tapping of the holes was done, and now men were already setting the heavy eyebolts and reeving the chains through, ready to hold the ship against the thrust of the great hydraulic jack he had placed astern of her. But still the tubes were too fat. If the ram was strong enough to force them in, the chains would part. He must reduce the resistance, but he saw no way to do it now except to heat the tubes, and that he was reluctant to do, for his tank soundings showed he was already dangerously short of fuel. They had expended it lavishly in their escape from Jupiter. There was barely enough liquid hydrogen to get them off the satellite and on their way to port, with a small margin over for the landing.

Benton shook his head when questioned as to possible sources of substitute fuel. All the uranium had been lost overboard when the feed pipes were broken with full pressure still behind the fuel supply. That had been necessary at the time, and it was fruitless to waste regrets on it now.

Bullard sat down and explored the ship mentally, checking off one by one the contents of the storerooms. There was nothing he could use that did not have some drawback. Ammonal there was plenty of, but he had doubts as to its safety. Then, suddenly, the solution hit him.

"Go ahead and set your first tube," he directed; "Number 1. Then send all the men you can spare into the nose blister—break out a couple of tons of that steel wool. That's what we will use."

It made a pretty blaze, that tube housing stuffed with steel wool saturated in liquid air, and a short one. Under the terrific outpouring of heat, the tube reddened and swelled, and the ready nose of the first of the bushings was jockeyed into the mouth of the tube and the great jack set in motion. Upward it drove, the ship straining against her leashes, but the pad-eyes set in the hard, planetary iron held, and the quivering *Pollux* had to receive her bushing. There was no evading the thrust of the ram.

One by one the other bushings were run in and rammed tight, and as the surrounding housing cooled, its contraction crushed the liner to as tight a fit as any yard in the Solar System could have achieved with all their fine equipment. Bullard had no misgivings as to their reliability. They would stay in place.

He was an hour ahead of schedule when the last tool was back on board and the warning howlers announced the imminent take-off. The *Pollux* spouted flame—old-fashioned flame, such as the *Asia* still used—then roared upward on her homeward flight.

"Send this, please," the admiral crisply commanded the tired but contented acting captain of the *Pollux*. Bullard looked at him in surprise. The radio had been repaired, but why did he want to send a signal? No one needed a tug now. They would be in in an hour—long before any tug could be warmed up. But he took the signal, since the admiral had offered it, and read. It was addressed to all ships and stations and began, "I have this day inspected the cruiser *Pollux* and find her ready in all respects for any contingency of the service—"

The first casualty of the trip really to hit Bullard occurred at that point. Something went wrong with his eyes, and for a moment the message in his fingers was just a blur. He saw the words "special commendation," and a mention of a Commander Bullard, and by then he had reached the familiar signature—Abercrombie. He did notice that the ship's score was a flat four-o, and at the moment that was all he cared about. She had made the grade.

AN OFFICER *who governs his command with morbid fidelity to regulations is not esteemed by his subordinates, nor does he have a "happy" ship—if ill fortune has promoted him to captain and made him the sole arbitrator of other men's actions. Mutiny is the unforgivable sin to be committed by the members of any service, but men may be driven to it as Captain Bligh's crew once testified. There were Captain Blighs in deep space also. And, on his very first tour of duty as executive officer, Commander Bullard had to deal with one, solving the problem in his own way.*

WHITE MUTINY

· For the first time in his life, Commander Bullard found himself dreading something—dreading it intensely. And, oddly enough, that something was no more than the routine Saturday inspection. In ten minutes he would buckle on his sword, that quaint ceremonial relic of antiquity, put on his awkward fore-and-aft hat, and accompany the new captain —Chinnery—through the mazes of the good spaceship *Pollux.*

He sighed helplessly, glanced up at Lieutenant Commander Fraser, thence let his eyes rove to the bookshelf where a fathom's length of canvas bound stood. He stared savagely at them. He had never realized before there were so many of them. Heretofore he had done his duty as he saw it and left chapter and verse to the sky lawyers.

But those fat books contained the awful clauses that regulated the conduct of the Space Guard. There they were —eight thick volumes—of the Regulations Proper. Ranged next were three volumes more of the Ordinance Instructions, and five of the Engineering Instructions. Then came the set relating to Astragation, and the fourteen learned tomes on Interplanetary Law; then the ones on Tactics and Strategy, then—

Bullard shuddered. It was overwhelming. To violate, even unwittingly, any provision contained in that compact library was technically "neglect of duty." And the new skipper was a hound for regulations.

"From here out," he had told Bullard the week before, on the occasion of his confiscation and destruction of all the crew's tailor-made liberty uniforms, "the regulations are in effect. *All* of them, not just the ones that happen to please you." And Bullard remembered the sullen faces of what had been a happy ship's company as they tossed their trim outfits into the incinerator door. A tapeline in Chinnery's own hands had revealed the clothing much too tight in the waist, and as much as three inches too full in the shoulders. It was, he said, a clear violation of Article 8878, sections B and D.

So they were destroyed. It did not seem to matter to

Chinnery that no self-respecting skyman would allow himself to be seen, even in the lowest dive, clad in the shoddy issue uniform, nor did it matter to him that each of those uniforms stood their owners two or three months' pay. They were non-reg, and that was that. What if the planet girls had a way of judging sailors by their clothes? What if the men sulked and grumbled at their work?

"A couple of days on bread and water will take that out of them," said Chinnery tartly when Bullard had protested. "The question is—are we going to run the ship the way the department wants it, or are we going to pamper the men?"

And Bullard thought back to the glowing report of their last admiral's inspection—that which had brought them all citations and promotions; and to the plaque in control that stated the *Pollux* to be the best all-round ship in the service. To a young man who had been taught that success lay in getting things done, that trophy seemed to be conclusive. Results, it seemed to him, were what counted, not the manner of the doing.

There was a rap at the door. It was the captain's orderly. Bullard took the folded paper he brought, read it, frowned, and tossed it onto the desk.

"Tell the captain I'll attend to it," he said to the orderly wearily. It was the umpty-umph message of the sort he had received in the past ten days.

"The captain said you were to answer forthwith in writing," said the orderly stiffly. His manner was punctiliously correct, yet there was the hint of insolence in the way he said it. Orderlies of man-baiting captains soon acquire the manner.

Bullard shot him a hard look, then reached for Volume 2 of the Regulations. The paper was upside down to Carlson, but he could read it.

FROM: Commanding Officer

TO: Executive Officer.

SUBJECT: Duties.

REFERENCE: Art. 2688, SS Regs.

1.   It has been brought to my attention that reference is not being complied with.

2.   You are directed to explain in writing at once the reasons for this dereliction in duty on your part.

CHINNERY.

Bullard found Article 2688, read it and gasped. It merely said: The executive officer shall wind the chronometer.

"Damnation," he muttered, and pushed the button for his yeoman. He dictated three terse sentences. The *Pollux's* chronometer behaved perfectly, it was wound daily by the assistant navigator, as was the practice in the fleet, the executive officer did not understand the commanding officer's allusion to dereliction in duty.

Bullard gnawed his lip while the yeoman rapped out the letter, then signed it and handed it without a word to the waiting orderly.

Within two minutes the orderly was back.

"The captain says," said the orderly, with even more of an undertone of insolence, "that he is not interested in the so-called customs of the service. He says that the regulations require the executive to wind the chronometer, and that there is nothing about delegating the duty to some subordinate. And that hereafter he wants straightforward answers to his memos, not evasive alibis."

Bullard glared at the man, the color mounting to his face. The orderly returned the look with a cool stare.

"He said you were to acknowledge the—"

"Get out of here!" roared Bullard, rising and thumping his desk.

"He's riding you, that's what, the dumb fathead!" exclaimed Fraser as the orderly disappeared down the passage. "He's still sore over the way you showed him up at that admiral's inspection. He's envious, he's yellow—"

"Easy!" warned Bullard. "After all, he's our superior officer."

"Superior, my eye!" snorted Fraser. "He's got more rank, yes. But it burns me up to even look at the slob. And every time I see that smart-aleck orderly I want to swing on him. That goes for that slippery ship's writer, too. Think of you having to wind the chronometer personally! Why, how—"

"How?" laughed Bullard harshly. "If you think that's something, look at this. He sent it in just before you came."

He tossed Fraser the earlier memo.

"*Phew!*" whistled the gunnery officer, popping his eyes.

"Yes," said Bullard bitterly. "Article 2751 says that the exec shall satisfy himself that the quarterly inventories are correct, but you see that his nibs construes that to mean an item-by-item personal check—and that doesn't mean sampling, either."

"What about all those firebricks in D-66? I used to do those by the cubic yard, but they are carried on the books by number—"

"I have to count 'em—the whole damn forty-two thousand some-odd of 'em."

"How will we ever get anything done?" asked Fraser blankly. He, like every other officer in the ship, had received his own quota of Captain Chinnery's curt queries as to this regulation and that. He had long since abandoned informal gunnery drills. All his gunner's mates were up to their necks, compiling lists of spare parts, motor serial numbers, and immersed in such other paper work.

"Thar she blows," remarked Bullard dully as the gong began to tap for quarters. He reached for his sword and cocked hat. "Well, let's go and get the bad news."

Bad news it was. Smug, plump little Chinnery stayed a long time in each compartment, blandly pointing out technical flaws. The only thing in the ship that seemed to please him were the ill-fitting, badly-dyed issue uniforms of the crew—made by the female convicts to kill time on bleak Juno. The disgruntled, sour looks of the men seemed not to disturb him at all. His ambition was to have the perfect ship—on paper—and his coup had been duly entered in the log. The reviewer in the department would read that and know of his zeal, whereas subtleties—like morale —were not so readily conveyed in cold type.

In sub-CC the inspecting party made its usual pause. The captain's eye lit on the old-style annunciator panel hung on the bulkhead above the intership communication board. He reached up and struck the glassite cover sharply with the heel of his hand. A black card bearing the number "24-B" dropped into view.

"What does that mean?" he barked at the unhappy operator, a recruit just come aboard. "What do you do when one of those drops?"

"I . . . I don't know, sir. N-nobody ever told me—"

"What!" squealed Chinnery. "Here you are, intrusted with the watch, and don't know what to do when a magazine is on fire? Bullard! What is the meaning of this?" He swung viciously on Bullard, puckering his fat face into what was meant to be a stern expression.

"That board—" began Bullard patiently. But Chinnery cut him off.

"Never mind that. *I* know what the board is. Why has not this man been instructed in his duties?"

"Because—" Bullard tried a second time, but the captain was not listening.

"Never mind the alibi. Yeoman! Take a note . . . for the commander's record . . . about this. Let's see, that makes Specification No. 14 under the charge of 'neglect of duty,' doesn't it?"

"Seventeen, sir," answered the yeoman, riffling through the pages of his notebook.

"Hm-m-m," muttered Chinnery.

"But—" objected Bullard, his wrath rising.

"But me no buts, young man. I am beginning to see that your vaunted efficiency was mostly luck. Imagine! Having a phone operator on watch who does not know what to do in case of a magazine fire!"

He turned to the now thoroughly frightened lad and, in what was meant to be a soothing voice, said:

"That, my boy, is an indicator of high magazine temperatures. If a number should ever drop, flood that magazine immediately—then notify me. The controls are to your right—there."

Bullard, purple with fury, restrained himself. Then he caught Fraser's solemn wink and decided to let it go. Fraser knew as well as he did that the board was no longer connected with the thermocouples in the powder storerooms. The dropping of a number could only mean that the board had been jarred, a thing that had occurred before, with embarrassing consequences. It was for that reason that this alarm system had been condemned and replaced by a better one in Central. That was why there was a job order on file for its complete removal the very next time they were back to the home yard on Luna.

Similar outbursts on the part of the captain took place in other spots, but it was not until they were inside the port torpedo rooms that his legalistic mind showed itself in its fullest flower. He laid his hand on a curious bulge in the inboard bulkhead.

"What is behind this?" he demanded.

"The original torpedo hoists," replied Fraser, "but we use the magnetic ones altogether now. These are blanked off with plating to keep dirt from accumulating in them."

"Ah," said Chinnery, "I seem to remember." He sent his yeoman scurrying back to the cabin for his file of quarterly reports. After he had returned, Chinnery turned his scowl on Fraser.

"More negligence," he said. "No routine tests, no monthly operating by hand, no quarterly reports for more than three years. No inventories or requisitions for spare parts. Don't the regulations mean *anything* to you?"

Fraser looked at his captain in blank amazement.

"Tut, tut," said Chinnery testily, "don't stand there like a gaping fool. The point is that the hoists are still installed, whether you use them or not. And since they are installed, they are subject to the usual maintenance routine and reports."

"But, captain," interposed Bullard, "the only reason they are still here is because, being obsolete, the department figured it was cheaper to abandon them in place and blank them in than to tear them out. Moreover, we can't run them monthly—the leads to the motors have been removed."

"Then run new ones," snapped the captain, "and replace the motors, if necessary."

"Aye, aye, sir," growled Bullard.

This was the last straw. If Chinnery kept this sort of thing up, the ship would be a raving madhouse before the month was out—absolutely ruined as a fighting ship. There is nothing that takes the spirit out of men and officers more than useless, foolish work—particularly when done at the expense of something truly worth while.

Bullard was soon to learn, however, that his troubles had just begun. In his capacity as executive officer, it fell to him to pass Chinnery's silly orders on to his juniors, who in their turn passed them on to the men, grumbling and venting themselves of caustic side remarks as they did. As for the men, they merely sulked, doggedly doing what they were told. Smoldering resentment was obvious everywhere, and it finally came to a head the day Chinnery slapped four men in the brig and put Lieutenant Carlson under hack for ten days. Their exact offense was not clearly understood, but the captain characterized it as "officiousness." They had done something on their own, not waiting for his direct order.

"But, commander," pleaded Fraser, "we can't go on this way. We had the finest ship in the whole damn service, but what have we got now? A madhouse! She's going to hell right under our noses. The men are on the verge of mutiny . . . both Benton and Tobelman have been disrated, a rank injustice . . . and I hear—"

"Yes, I know," replied Bullard morosely. He sat a moment in a brown study. He knew that a round robin was being circulated, that committees of petty officers had been formed, and that there were rocks ahead.

"Get those men up here," said Bullard suddenly, "and Carrick, too, the pharmacist."

When they came, Bullard looked them over steadily as they lined up before his desk. He knew them well, and they him. They were the mainstay of the ship—the real leaders of the crew—the men upon whom the officers depended to get things done. Men like those could make or break a captain. Bullard read their faces and thought back gratefully to a certain gruff old bos'n who had tactfully deflated him when he was a fresh-caught snotty. Some of that off-the-record discipline from beneath upward had been hard to take, but he knew now that he was a better officer for it.

"Men," he said, looking straight at them, "we have a tough assignment. We have a new captain. He is . . . well, *different* from Captain Dongan. He is more . . . er . . . regulation-minded, if you know what I mean."

"Yes, sir," chorused the men, "we know."

"The refuge of an incompetent," blurted out Fraser indignantly. "He knows damn well that as long as he sticks to the book they can't hang him, no matter what happens to the ship. But just let somebody exercise a little initiative, a little common sense, and right away his neck is in a bight. It *might* turn out wrong. He's yellow, I tell you. Bah!"

"An outburst like that may relieve the emotions, Fraser," said Bullard calmly, "but it does not alter the situation. Captain Chinnery is still the skipper, and as such he is much more than a man. He is a symbol . . . the symbol of the supreme authority. Moreover, every order he has issued has been strictly legal. Any refusal on our part to carry them out merely ruins us and hurts him not at all. We have no choice but to comply."

"And see the ship go merrily to hell!" Fraser was outraged.

"Perhaps."

It was then that Fraser and the three silent enlisted men first noted the half smile playing on Bullard's lips and the fleeting twinkle in his eye.

"Supposing," remarked Bullard dryly, fixing his eyes on the rows of books, "it does. There will be an investigation, naturally. Blame will be fixed. They always start at the top. I propose to let them stop there. I, for one, do not mean to accept the buck."

"Meaning?"

"Meaning that the only possible course open to us is cooperation."

"Cooperation?" Fraser's laugh was hard and dry. Benton and his comrades remained silent.

"Exactly. Captain Chinnery complains of misplaced initiative. Well, let's cut out initiative. He wants a 'reg' ship. Let's bone the book—turn sky lawyers. Let's do what we're told—*and not one damn thing more!*"

Bullard let his glance drift back to the three stolid men and the flushed officer before him. He noted Benton and Tobelman as they wiped the grins from their faces, and saw Fraser's hot indignation fade as comprehension dawned.

"Not bad . . . not bad," said the latter slowly. "Fight fire with fire, eh?"

"We'll pass the word, sir," came from Benton, and the other two men grinned frankly then, "cooperation it will be."

"Good," said Commander Bullard, and promptly immersed himself in Volume 2 of Regulations. None but a god, omnipotent and with all eternity to do it in, could expect to do all the things required of an executive officer, but he could try, paragraph by paragraph, just as they came. He looked at 2707.

> From time to time, the executive officer shall satisfy himself, by personal inspection, that boat boxes are in order—

"Ah," breathed Bullard, "I'll beat him to that one." And he walked out onto the broad fin where the boats were cradled. One hundred and nineteen items in each boat box— and there were eight boats! It would take two days' work, that simple duty alone!

It was about two weeks after that that the rumors began to fly about the revival of banditry on Neptune. Only spaceships could cope with them, for over that jagged and precipitous terrain and in that airless sky the usual planetary gendarmerie could not operate effectively. The scuttlebutt was more and more persistent that one of the larger ships of the Jovian Patrol was about to be detached and sent there to wipe the villains out.

Bullard made a wry face when he heard of it, for the most likely ship was, of course, the *Pollux*. Ironically enough, Admiral Abercrombie's last report of her unequivocally pronounced her to be the ship best fitted for emergency duty. Yet Bullard knew, as every man jack aboard— unless Chinnery himself be excepted—that the *Pollux* of a scant four months before was a thing of the past, a legend. Morale? It was to laugh! Or weep.

Only three days before, the starboard condenser had sprung a leak, and when it was reported to the captain he went to have a look.

"Well, pull it down and roll in that tube," he snapped.

Benton's men turned to, pulled it down, and rolled the tube. Then they replaced the shell, laboriously made all the connections and put it back in service. An hour later two more tubes went.

"Hell's bells!" squealed Chinnery when they told him. "How can that be? You were in that condenser only yesterday. Couldn't you see those other two tubes were about to go?"

"You told us to roll the leaky one, sir," said Benton, his face the ultimate in dead pan. He might have added that it was not the tubes that were at fault, but a warped header. But he was not asked that.

"Such stupidity!" muttered Captain Chinnery. "Very well, yank it down again and do it all over."

"The one we did yesterday?" asked Benton, registering faint surprise.

"No, fool, the two that just blew out!"

"Yes, sir."

Bullard looked on impassively. Chinnery's tart words of a few weeks past still burned. "When I want anything done, I'll order it—this ship is not so complicated that one man can't do the thinking for it."

Yet, as he recalled that, knowing that that very morning the condenser had been pulled down for the third time, he wondered just how the *Pollux* could get to Neptune, if ordered, and what she could do if she got there. Bullard shrugged and dismissed the matter from his mind. That was Chinnery's worry. Then he looked up to see the goat-getting orderly standing by his desk with the inevitable memorandum in his hand.

Listlessly Bullard took it and read:

> In view of our probable departure shortly for one of the outer planets, you will take such action as may be necessary to insure that no contraband is brought on board. Section 10,009, SS Regs.

Bullard straightened up in his chair and frowned. He knew without looking what the reference was—it was the *one* article in the book that even the most arrant martinet found it expedient to ignore. That is, where Neptune and Pluto were concerned. For Martian *joola-joola*, the forbidden beverage, was the only known specific against the mysterious and invisible radiations emanated by those cold and rocky dim planets. Out there it did not intoxicate—it was a vital stimulant. Yet since the control board were Puritanical Earthlings, the space guard had never been able to have the article modified. Hence the unwritten law of the service that its breach must be winked at.

The young exec knew that the returning liberty party would be well heeled with the stuff—cleverly enough concealed to save the face of the O.D., who, at least, had to go through the motions of upholding the regulations. He glanced at the clock. It was well after five, Io time, and shortly boats would start coming back. He got up uneasily and walked out toward the exit port. He had learned something about Chinnery's methods and he feared dirty work of some sort.

"What is that gadget?" Bullard asked of Ensign Pitto, the officer of the deck, pointing to a contraption being erected in the gangway.

"A field fluoroscope, sir. Captain's orders. They are setting up the x-ray tube behind that sheet of canvas across the passage."

Bullard scowled at the layout, then hurried to his office. Lately he had learned to suppress anger, but at the moment it was hard. For he saw instantly through the captain's malicious plan. Apparently Chinnery, when it suited his purposes, knew how to evade the regulations, too. To be sure he was right, Bullard snatched down the volume entitled "Pertaining to Enlisted Personnel." Yes, it was there. The men had *some* rights.

14,075: Neither the person nor the effects of any enlisted man may be searched except upon good and sufficient grounds. Except in cases of suspected theft, and where a man has a known bad record, a man's own statement that he possesses no contraband shall be deemed sufficient—

"So," he murmured grimly, "a search that is not a search. A slinking, slimy way to smear the records of hundreds of men—and to hang me on the rebound." He slammed the book shut. "Well—he'll do neither."

Twenty minutes later, Bullard jumped out of one of the gyrocopters that were acting as tenders for the ship. The landing stage was still empty, but soon it would be full of returning skymen, their arms full of bundles—innocent purchases—and somewhere else upon them the forbidden *joola-joola*. And out at the ship, Captain Chinnery waited craftily with his trap all set.

"Hold the next boat for the ship until I get back," Bullard said hastily to Lieutenant Carlson, who was handling the beach guard. With that he dashed off to the nearest liquor dive.

On his way he passed a number of the *Pollux's* men, heading for the boat landing. They saluted sheepishly, still painfully self-conscious for having to wear the unsightly issue uniforms that made them pariahs on shore.

By the time he reached the liquor joint, though, it was empty. Or almost. In one corner, almost concealed by a post, sat the captain's yeoman—Ship's Writer Norvick. As the door slammed behind Bullard, he saw the yeoman fold up a notebook and slide it into a pocket. Ranged on the bar stood a row of flat curved-glass bottles, most of them empty. The bartender was filling the others from a huge demijohn of the delicate violet *joola-joola*.

"Aha," thought Bullard, "check and double check, eh? Chinnery's chief spy is getting the dope at the source!"

He turned abruptly and strode from the place. He had seen enough. The belly flasks lined up on the bar told him how the stuff was being smuggled. The presence of the skipper's snooping yeoman, coupled with the waiting x-ray machine at the gangway of the *Pollux*, told him how the captain had planned to trip him up—and most of the crew with him.

He bounded toward the landing stage, inwardly raging. But his anger did not cloud his thought. At every step he turned over some new plan for defeating the captain's scheme. He was actuated, as he had been when he had pro-posed non-cooperative cooperation to forestall overt mutiny, by the highest motives. He wanted to save the crew—and the junior officers—from their small-minded incompetent captain. Constantly goaded as they were by picayune quibbling and nagging, he was fearful of an out-right rupture. And in that event everybody would lose.

It was a situation he found galling, for, like the crew, he was capable of the fiercest loyalty—if properly led. It was unfortunate that out of such a generally splendid serv-ice the crack crew of the *Pollux* should draw a weak sister for a captain, a man who hid his lack of ability behind the

technicalities of the printed word. But it had. The thing to
do was make the best of it.

Bullard's heart fell when he reached the landing stage.
Carlson had finished his superficial inspection and already
loaded the men into the boat, which stood waiting to shove
off. That was bad, for if it could be proved that the men had
carried the liquor into one of the ship's tenders it was the
same as having taken it on board the *Pollux* herself.
Bullard's plan for warning the men while still beyond the
jurisdiction of the space guard was unworkable. And as
he saw the yeoman Norvick had come along behind him,
he knew that calling the liberty party back ashore so they
could get rid of the contraband would be worse than doing
nothing. Like a flash, he changed his plans.

"Out of the boat, all you men, and fall in on the dock.
Single rank."

Several of the waiting men blinked in surprise at the
order, but they got out of the boat and fell in.

"I have orders," said Bullard slowly, "to see that no
contraband goes aboard. But before I question you on that
score, I will make a brief uniform inspection."

He turned around to where a patrolman stood behind
him twirling an oak nightstick.

"Lend me that a moment," said Bullard, and took the
stick.

He paused before the first man in line and looked him
up and down. The skin-tight issue trousers afforded no
hiding place for anything. Yes, it must be all in belly

flasks. Thoughtfully he extended the club and gently tapped the rigid skyman on his blouse, just above the middle. There was a faint clink.

Pam! With a quick and unexpected stroke, Bullard brought the stick down harder. Then he stepped on to the next man. Behind him he thought he heard the *tinkle-tinkle* of glass fragments raining on the pavement, but he did not look back. Again the tentative tap, again the sharp, sudden blow, again the muffled crash—and a slowly widening damp spot on the barbarous issue uniform. Bullard did not give it a glance, but stepped forward. Somewhere in the background someone snickered, but the young exec's face was a study in nonexpression.

Fourteen times down that line he detected the telltale clink, and fourteen times he swatted. Then he stood back, looking the men in the face, not at the small, widening puddles of violet something at their feet.

"Have any of you men any contraband substance in your possession?"

"No, sir!"

The yell was in unison, as if previously rehearsed. Bullard's face almost cracked into a wide grin, but he managed to get the better of it.

"Embark!" he said.

The men got back into the boat, Norvick among them. Bullard was about to follow when he saw a fresh group of men coming down the dock, Benton and Carrick among them. Bullard walked to meet them.

"When you get aboard, Carrick," said Bullard in the

most matter-of-fact way, "you had better check up on the operation of your x-ray-fluoroscope outfit. Captain Chinnery is using it at the gangway."

"The sunnuva—" began Carrick.

"Pipe down!" growled Benton to Carrick. Then to the commander, "Thank you, sir; we'll be coming out in the next boat."

"Splendid," said Bullard, and there was just the slightest little jerk of his right eyelid. Benton wheeled and spread out his arms to the group of skymen assembling for the boat.

"Back, men. I want to talk to you."

"Shove off," said Bullard to the coxswain, settling himself among the slightly damp and odoriferous men he had just inspected. He shot one look at the ship's writer sitting opposite him with a crooked little smile on his face, as if he was sucking the marrow out of some private joke, then looked out at the fleeting Ionian landscape. He shrugged. There was no contraband in *this* boat. Nor, in so far as anybody could prove, had ever been.

"You're hair-splitting, Bullard, and that is all there is to it!"

Chinnery was fairly screaming with rage. "You should have arrested those men, confiscated the bottles for evidence, and brought them to me to—"

"My orders," said Bullard, struggling for calm expression, "said to take such action as may be necessary to prevent contraband being brought aboard. To the best of my knowledge, none was. Those orders are in my safe, awaiting the court of inquiry the *Pollux* is certain to have before—"

"The court-martial *you* are sure to have!" yelped the captain. "For I have an independent witness who saw those flasks of *joola-joola*—"

"Saw flasks filled with a pale-violet liquid," corrected Bullard coolly. "Unhappily, they were flimsy flasks, and the stuff is lost. There is no way to prove what was in them. So far as I know, it was that perfume they make from the Ganymedean *plimris* bloom."

A boat bell clanged.

"Never mind," said Chinnery, triumph supplanting his petulant anger, "step with me to the gangway. The moment I heard of your pusillanimous behavior I sent a message to the beach guard that there were to be no more belly-patting inspections."

Bullard followed along with considerably mixed feelings. He had the utmost reliance on Benton's quickness of perception and on his versatility. What fruit had the veiled warning he had thrown out brought?

"Here are three of them," said Ensign Pitto, motioning toward the three skymen lined up against the bulkhead. "The rest were clean."

"Aha!" gloated Chinnery, shooting an I-told-you-so look at the discomfited Bullard.

The three men were the three outstanding petty officers of the ship—Benton, Tobelman, and Carrick. Chinnery stooped and squinted at the fluoroscope. Bullard could not help seeing, too. Each of the men had a flat, rectangular package under his jacket athwart his navel. The shape was unmistakable—*joola-joola* bottles! Made of lead glass, they showed up like a sore thumb.

"Search them—strip them!" yelled the captain, sure of his victory.

"Sir, we protest." It was Benton who spoke. "We pledge our word we have no contraband. You have no right—"

"Carry out my orders!" screamed the captain, turning in fury on the bos'n's mate of the watch.

In a moment the jackets were ripped away and the flask-shaped objects snatched out of the tight belts of the three protesting men.

"W-w-what the—" Captain Chinnery turned one of them over and over in his hands, absolutely nonplused. The slab was slightly curved and of a sort of plaster. On the face of it was a crude bas-relief of a heifer and a scribbled inscription reading, "Souvenir of the Ionian Barium Mines, made of one of our products—gamma-ray-resisting barium plaster."

For a moment Captain Chinnery stood stupidly staring at the thing he was twisting in his hands. Then he dashed it to the deck and strode off down the passage, combing his hair with agitated fingers and muttering, "Damn, damn, damn!" Bullard looked after the departing figure and began to laugh. In an instant the whole corridor was reverberating with the howls of twenty laughing men as the next boatload of men poured through the port and down toward their lockers. Ensign Pitto, mystified and baffled by the

entire proceedings, looked wonderingly on, not bothering
to use the now discredited fluoroscope again.

Benton picked up his plaster objet d'art and stuck it back
under his belt.

"Somebody owes me a quart," he said to a man passing.

"You'll get it," said the man. "Two of 'em."

The precipitous walls of Nereus Crater ringed them like
a huge Coliseum. The face of every man in the control
room of the *Pollux* was set in hard, grim lines. They were
anxious, and many of them wondered whether they had
been so smart, after all. For they were hurtling straight
downward toward the ragged cone in the center at hideous
velocity, and every one of them knew the ship about them
was a semiwreck. Half her engine room was torn apart—
for routine tests—and the same applied to her battery. She
could hardly be worked. It was problematical whether she
could be fought. And in this crater were said to be more
than a thousand of the toughest rascals who ever slit a
throat.

Yet as each man turned over in his mind his own contribution to the chaos, he could not help recall some saying
of the captain. Throughout the cramped room, through the
mind of one or another of them, ran the memory of such
curt and devastating sayings as these—all quotations from
Captain Chinnery:

"When I want information, I'll ask for it."

"I'm long on ideas, young man. All I expect of you is
execution."

"Never mind why—I tell you to do it."

"Of course it handicaps gunfire—but the regulations call for it."

"Cancel the drill—you have three quarterly reports to get out."

"You exceed your authority! Wait for orders hereafter!"

And on and on. You were damned if you did, damned if you didn't. When a man cannot be pleased, nobody tries.

Captain Chinnery set the counterblasts to raging, and the fall of the ship was checked with a shudder. Fraser was searching the horizon for the bandit lair. Then of a sudden the roar of the exhaust sputtered and stopped. Chinnery angrily barked into the engine-room communicator:

"Who stopped those motors?"

"Fuel exhausted, sir."

Chinnery paled. No one spoke, but all knew the inevitable answer. And the cause. They would crash, for the hydrogen tubes could not be limbered up in time. And the reason for it was that Chinnery had refused to okay the last uranium requisition on the ground the ship had already exceeded her quarterly allowance!

Chinnery threw in the antigravity units, but they were weak and it was too late. The *Pollux* struck, at somewhere about ninety miles an hour, bounced high in the airless sky, then struck again, nose down. The lights went out, then came on. Men picked themselves up, nursing bruises, and looked at one another and the disordered compartments about them.

"Fire in all magazines!" came the startling announcement over the loud-speakers. "Magazines flooded."

Bullard groaned. His non-cooperative cooperation had gone farther than he meant it to.

Pasted on the annunciator board in sub-CC were the captain's orders—to flood whenever any of those unconnected monitors showed! The jar of falling had brought them all down, of course, and the operator following the rule of blind obedience had done as he was told. The ship's guns were useless.

Chinnery looked sick, but he still had a grip on himself.

"Get up torpedoes," he directed. "Seeing us like this, they may attack at any moment."

"Can't," said Fraser without making any bones of it. "No hoists working."

"What!" bleated Chinnery.

"Right. You wanted those original ones operated—for the record. Well, we did. But to do it we had to rob the real hoists of their motors. It'll take another day to get them back again."

A bell began a clamorous clanging.

"A number of men headed this way across the crater floor," sang out the lookout. "There are tanks with them, and a caterpillar gun of some kind."

"Do something, Bullard," said Chinnery in a pleading voice, turning white-faced to his young exec. "You're a resourceful fellow."

"I am at your command, captain," said Bullard stiffly. "What is it you wish me to do?"

"They are setting that gun," the lookout informed them. "It's due west of us—nearly astern, as we lie. The men on foot are deploying at the foot of the slope."

"Fit out the landing force," managed Chinnery, finding his voice after the third gulp.

"Sorry," said Bullard, "but the small-arms magazine is flooded. Our ray guns are in there, too. There are no weapons available, unless it's the cutlery in the galley. Your order, you know—nothing ever to be left out of magazines."

The ship shuddered. There was a quick succession of staccato reports as a metallic hail beat against her armored sides. The brigands' gun was getting the range.

"The party on foot has a heat gimlet," reported the lookout. "They are working their way around to the north."

"Commence firing!" squeaked Chinnery. He was near to fainting.

"What with?" asked Fraser, having no wish to spare him.

Suddenly Chinnery got a grip on himself and straightened up. Wildly he looked around at the silent, accusing, unhelpful faces. Then he addressed Bullard.

"You win, Bullard. From the very first I recognized it would be you or me. But organized mutiny is too much. I yield—for the good of the ship. Take over. Do it your way." His voice trailed away. Then he drooped across the chart rack and vomited. "Black mutiny," he muttered, over and over again. "Black mutiny and insubordination."

Bullard's lip curled in scorn.

"What order of yours was ever refused? What threat was ever made you? And now, after you've wrecked us, you want to quit. Because you don't know what to do. You're yellow!"

Bullard glared at the cringing figure.

"But," he went on, not regarding the now persistent hail of pellets against the hull, "under your precious library of rules, you *can't* quit. Not while you are alive and well. The captain cannot duck his responsibility—not ever!"

"I'm a sick man," wailed Chinnery, sliding to the deck.

Bullard jerked his head toward the surgeon, Lieutenant Herilon.

"He's sick, all right," said Herilon after an examination of about one second. "Diagnosis: blue funk. Prognosis: terrible. In other words, he's unfit for duty."

"Very well, then," said Bullard. "I'll take over. But, doc, be sure that gets in the log."

The doc grinned. The ship had gotten regulation-minded, all right.

Bullard went into action like a prodded bobcat.

"Benton! Warm up those old stern tubes and get ready to shoot measured blasts.

"Harris! Break out those two heavy jacks and take 'em outside. Set one on each side of the ship and slue her around until our stern bears on that bandit gun.

"Tobelman! Wangle half a dozen of your torps out of their brackets, stick 'em on dollies and manhandle 'em the best way you can to the rocket room.

"Carlson, you compute the ballistic. I'm firing torpedoes that way. You know the Neptune gravity, and there's a vacuum outside. Benton'll give you the pressure tables."

"The tubes are bigger than the torps," said Carlson.

"I know. Build up your torps with wire-rope grommets until they fit!"

Bullard paused for breath. Then he saw Norvick, slightly green about the gills, huddled in a corner.

"You—captain's yeoman! Grab your notebook and get busy." Bullard's voice was harsh and his eye was hard. "I want you to put down every breach of the regulations that happens from now on. Begin with the one—whatever its number is—that says you can't divert engineering material to the use of the ordinance department. And mind you, if you miss a single one, you're up for a court!"

"Yes, sir," whimpered the amazed ship's writer, but he dragged out his bulky notebook.

The lookout was reporting again.

"Those men are about halfway up the hill now. They have some other machine with them—can't make it out."

"Fraser!" shouted Bullard. "How long will it take you to convert that big exhaust blower in the topside fin to a centrifugal machine gun? Do you know what kind of an animal that is?"

"Yes, sir. I do. About five shakes of a lamb's tail!"

"Get at it. Only do it in four."

"Aye, aye, sir. But ammunition?"

"There are three or four tons of assorted ball bearings in storeroom D-60. I'll see that you get 'em."

In a couple of minutes Bullard ceased bellowing orders. He wiped his eyes and shook his head. He was beginning to feel queer, sickly sensations. Of a sudden a dread came over him that at any moment he would cave in. He took a deep breath, but it did no good. Then he noticed his hands were trembling.

"The radiations are getting bad, sir," reported the doctor. "Several men have caved in already. I'm administering *suprene*, but it does not seem to be very effective."

Bullard knew then what had gone wrong with him.

"Don't waste time with that stuff," he said impatiently. "Serve out a slug of *joola-joola* all around."

"There's none on board," said Herilon. "I tried—"

"The hell there isn't! There's gallons of it. Just ask Carrick, or Tobelman, or—"

Herilon had gone, on the jump.

The ship shook. That time it was from her own recoil. Carlson had shot his first torpedo from the stern rocket tubes. There was a moment's wait for the spot, then a second one went.

"That group's through," reported Carlson gleefully a moment later. "Boy! What a mess those torps do make!"

"Help Fraser with the other crowd."

Ten minutes later, fortified by a double shot of *joola-joola*, Bullard watched the terrible execution on the down-slope to starboard. First there was the singing whine as the high-speed motor worked up to velocity, then the rattle as the hopperful of ball bearings fell against the swift-revolving vanes. Then, under the wide-flung hail of that super-

colossal blunderbuss, the oncoming pirates crumpled. Their
mystery machine stood a moment later alone and untended
in the midst of their piled-up corpses.

"That seems to be all of them," said Bullard. "Tell
Benton to stand by to pull out of this hole with the old
rockets. We'll get more uranium as soon as we get to base."

Admiral Mike Dongan lifted his eyebrows at the mass of
paper Bullard laid before him. Old Captain Mike, after his
promotion, had been sent to the outer zone as force commander. So it was to him, in Tethys Advanced Base, that
Bullard reported.

"But—" puzzled the old man. Bullard had never gone
in heavily for paper work when he knew him on the *Pollux*.

"That first stack," explained Bullard, "are the accumu-
lated charges against me up to the moment I took temporary
command—"

"Bosh," said Admiral Mike Dongan, glancing over the
topmost sheet. He dumped the lot in the wastebasket.

"The other stack lists the things I did wrong to get the
old *Pollux* out of the hole. I never knew until—"

"Really?" said Captain Mike, more attentive. He slid
open a drawer of his desk and carefully laid the damning
documents inside. "These are more to the point. I want to
forward these to the control board." He shut the drawer,
then locked it.

Bullard did not know exactly what reaction those papers
were going to bring, but certainly he had not anticipated
that. It was disconcerting.

"You see," said Admiral Mike, studying the curling smoke from his cigar, "I have been authorized to prepare another volume of the Regulations—"

Bullard winced.

"—to be entitled 'Instructions for Procedure in Extraordinary Emergencies' "—the admiral kept tugging at another drawer—"umph . . . and this . . . umph . . . is just the sort of thing we want for it."

By then the old man had the drawer open, and out of it he fished a gleaming crystal beaker half filled with the aromatic forbidden juice of Mars. He filled two glasses with the violet liqueur.

"Of course, before Captain Chinnery was put on the retired list this morning, he did submit quite a lengthy list of your . . . er . . . *derelictions*, I believe he called them—"

"Yes?" said Bullard, on tenterhooks.

"Here's to 'em," said the admiral, hoisting his glass, and admiring the delicate color. He took a sip.

"But fourteen charges and who knows how many specifications—"

"Nobody gives a damn," said the admiral with great decision. "You got the bandits, didn't you—all of 'em? You brought the *Pollux* in, didn't you? Drink hearty, boy— you've got my old job. You're skipper of the *Pollux* now!"

A SPY *is a hero in his own country, and sometimes to die wearing another man's uniform is the height of bravery. But to come home safely again with the "goods" is even better.*

Captain Bullard had had his dream of what his first command would be (as what space officer has not). He never expected to take out a rusty tramp freighter. But the Service had a last ditch hope, Intelligence had a scheme (which Bullard added to), and he was the one to volunteer for the unenviable role of blockade runner.

BLOCKADE RUNNER

·"Thar she blows!"

While the alarm jangled, Red Leary, the quartermaster, cocked an eye at the pulsating ruby pick-up light, noted the bearing, and then laid a hand on the jet-feed cut-off valve. He looked expectantly at the skipper.

"Hold it," cautioned the latter, "until they challenge. Sparks! Is your board manned?"

"Aye, sir."

"Rebel cruiser coming up on the port quarter. He'll be calling in a minute. Don't chance talking to him—stick to

101

code. I'm just a little afraid of your dialect. One slip and we're done."

The call came almost instantly, strident and insistent. First it was QF, QF, QF, and on the heels of that came the peremptory BWB—"What ship?" "Heave to, to receive boarding party."

" 'Vast blasting," ordered Bullard. "Tell 'em okay, Sparks."

Red's hand moved. The *Cloud Queen* trembled, then lurched backward as she dropped her acceleration. The three men looked at one another. Here it was; in another half-hour, at most, they would know. Their elaborate masquerade was about to be tested. They would know the answers to a lot of questions. Whether they would meet the unknown fate of the fourteen ships that had preceded them; whether the Martian-Jovian blockade was really unbreakable; whether they were to live or die; whether, indeed, there was a chance left for the Earth Empire to live or die. Red swallowed hard, while Sparks moistened his lips with a nervous tongue. Bullard, the skipper, was surveying the room critically, on the alert for any item, hitherto overlooked, that might arouse suspicion. Seeing nothing, he relaxed. The stage was set—from now on it must be acting.

No one who had formerly known John Bullard, resourceful and trim captain of the Tellurian Space Force, would have recognized him as he appeared at that moment. His face was all but covered by a newly grown, fierce black beard that had been artfully threaded with gray by the experts of the chromosurgery section of Intelligence. It matched the equally artificial grayness of his temples. The deep tan of the ray-burned spaceman was not synthetic, but somehow seemed to be set off and augmented by the threadbare old uniform trimmed in tattered, greenish-gold lace. In every inch he looked to be what he was pretending to be—the somewhat bedraggled skipper of a second-rater out of Venus. The crew as well, likewise ratings of the Space Force, were similarly disguised.

As for the ship, no one familiar with the well-found ships of the Cosmos Line would ever guess that this dingy vessel was in reality the *Violet*, well known before the war along the Saturnian run. Her metamorphosis had been as thorough as that of the men in her, thanks to the creative imaginations and the accurate memories of a dozen operatives at Lunar headquarters.

No detail of hull, equipment or cargo had been overlooked. The framed register screwed to the bulkhead in the cabin was puckered and stained with ugly brown water marks, as if a negligent quartermaster had left the lock doors open while cradled in the steamy atmosphere of her home port. The crew's quarters were decorated with intimate snapshots of alluring females taken against the fantastic background of Venusian scenery. Every man on board was not only provided with forged licenses and passports, but with personal correspondence written in many hands on the damp-proof paper of Venus and bearing appropriate stamps and cancellations. Outside, clinging to every irregularity in the hull, were patches of the hardy

Venusian moss that thrives even in the void, planted there
by a crafty technician from London's great interplanetary
botanical garden. And, of course, bolted to the hull just
over the ship's nose was the inevitable hemi-cylinder
housing the infrared headlight by which the master could
find his way through the misty ceiling down to the landing
field of Aphrodite's Haven. If anywhere among all that
artistry there was a single flaw, it was not from want of
foresight or trying.

A slight shudder marked the coming alongside of the
cruiser's boat. Bullard pushed the switch that turned on the
lights in the lock and loosed the guard on the outer door.
Then he reached up and plucked from its brackets a Mark
IX Heimlitz blaster—the sporting model. Sticking that into
his holster, he walked along the passage to greet his ad-
versary.

He knew from the clang of the outer door and the hissing
of air that the boarders were already in the lock. In a
moment the door burst open and a scowling officer stepped
out, followed closely by two bluejackets with drawn ray
guns of the latest heavy-duty model. Bullard knew at a
glance they were Callistans from the silver lozenges em-
broidered on their uniforms. Only a Callistan would wear
such a device. In the beginning, when Callisto was a Tellurian penal colony, lozenges were woven into the cloth
of their garments as the stigmata of criminality. Yet so
shameless is that race that upon gaining their independence
ten years ago, they adopted the lozenge as their national

insignia and thereafter flaunted it openly throughout the system.

"Jig's up," said the Callistan briefly as he stepped into the ship. Without ceremony, he snatched the blaster from Bullard's belt and handed it to one of his men. "Save the act until later," he added contemptuously as Bullard jumped backward, registering indignant astonishment. Then he turned on his heel and strode toward the control room. Bullard followed, silent and perturbed. The boarding officer was not going to be an easy man to deal with.

"Swell job of camouflage," commented the Callistan after a quick inspection of the control room. "If they had faked your first ships like this, you might have got by with one of them." He studied Bullard insolently, and then, "Okay, buddy. Go into your song and dance now—I'm listening. It's been dull out here, waiting for you, and we need a laugh. And I hope you've thought up a new one. The gag about being an innocent Venusian merchantman just trying to get along in the Universe has been worked to a frazzle. But shoot, anyway. Only make it short and snappy, because I already know the answer."

Bullard shrugged his shoulders and spread his hands in a gesture of hopelessness. So far the Callistan was bluffing, and Bullard knew it.

"What else can I tell you? But look us over—our papers —our holds—everything, if you doubt us."

"Doubt you?" roared the big Callistan with a hearty laugh. "Why, Mr. Tellurian Space Force Whatever-your-rank-is, I haven't *any* doubt about you. There's a couple of things I don't *know* about you—like what your real name is—but out at the mines that won't matter. They'll give you a number, anyway."

He started his search methodically, missing nothing, however trifling. He thumbed through the log, squinted at the makers' nameplates on each bit of astragational gear, scratched the mold-resisting paint to see what was under it, and sniffed the air appraisingly. Thanks to the still-hanging fumes of huil-huil, it had a thorough-going Venusian aroma. He glanced at the big jar of crushed, dried huil-huil leaves sitting on the radioman's desk. Not more than a handful of the weed so prized by space-going Venusians was gone from the jar—no more than half a dozen men could smoke in the day or so since the *Cloud Queen,* as she claimed, had escaped internment at Luna Base.

The flat, brutal face lit up with that I-told-you-so joy, and he pointed triumphantly at the nearly full jar.

"An empty one might have fooled me," he fairly shouted, "but now I've seen all I want to see. You guys always overdo your stuff. Look, stupid—you been interned on Luna, where you can't get that weed—a year, you say—locked up all the time in your ship. And then, two days ago, you hop off all hunky-dory with a nice full jar. I ask you. How does that add up?"

Bullard smiled patiently, letting his meticulously yellowed teeth show through his beard.

"My friend, you are too, too suspicious. We have tons of it. In the hold you will find ten thousand pounds. Look in the manifest; it is part of our cargo—bound for your country, for Ganymede. It is true we have swiped a few hundred pounds for our own use, a matter we will have to settle for with the consignee, but our laws permit us to make use of cargo in an emergency. And being captured by those accursed Earthmen is an emergency."

The Callistan looked a little dubious, but he accepted the manifest and the invoices. He looked through them and then went on a tour of the ship. For an hour he prowled through the cargo spaces, but nowhere could he find any irregularity. They were filled with products of Venus, all articles of common commerce with the Jovian satellites. Nor could he find any indication of concealed armaments. The ship was plainly no Q-boat, as a quick look at the engine room proved. There was only the usual auxiliary generating equipment. The ship could not possibly be made into a commerce raider.

Back in the control room, the boarding officer dropped his taunting, bullying air and listened more politely to Bullard's story, although it was clear he was reluctant to release the vessel and permit her to complete her voyage.

Bullard kept on talking, telling of his hard luck at being picked up during the very first week of the war, and of the hardships of internment, of the pitiful inadequacy of the Tellurian fleet and the incapacity of its officers, and of the general state of despair prevailing on the Moon. He also

made much of the fact that he had successfully resisted all
efforts to take the cargo out of his ship and put it to use on
the grounds that it would be a violation of Venus' neu-
trality and might force her into war on the other side.

The Callistan frowned, obviously in a quandary. He was
still unconvinced. He had uncovered nothing that was not
plausible, yet nothing he had seen could not have been
faked. He meant to take no chances on letting a prize slip
through his fingers. Yet he knew that Venus was opposed to
this resumption of the war and was itching for an excuse
to patch up her differences with the mother planet and
come to her aid. Bullard sensed his hesitation, and by an
almost imperceptible twitch of an eyelid got the signal
across to Red Leary. The time had come to play their
trump.

Red's freckle-specked hand stole behind him and
fumbled for a button. On the third try he managed to trip
the latch on a small cupboard, the one where the star charts
were ordinarily kept. Bullard went on talking, pleading
now to be allowed to go on to his destination.

"Hell and damnation!" yelled the Callistan, leaping
frantically. Something disreputably ragged-looking and
dirty white was clinging to a wildly kicking calf.

"So sorry," cried Bullard in dismayed apology, and
dived for it. For a moment he was busy dodging the boarding officer's scuffling knees, but after a false grab or two he
came up clutching a queer and malodorous little animal by
the scruff of the neck. "I should have warned you about
Flo-Flo. She doesn't like strangers."

The creature was a full-grown trigglemouse, one of those feathered rodents peculiar to Venus. For some reason unfathomed by the remainder of the inhabitants of the Solar System—unless it was blind superstition—the men of Venus cherished the beasts. No ship from there ever took the void without one as a mascot. Yet they stank and they stole and they nipped friend and foe alike with their sharp, chiselly teeth, and they had other habits that, to say the least, were not nice. In fact, the aversion to them was so strong among most Earthmen that when Flo-Flo was requisitioned, all the zoos of the Earth had to be combed before she could be located.

The Callistan glowered for a long time after he had blasted the miserable animal out of existence, but as his curses died away it was obvious enough that whatever lingering doubts he may have had as to the authenticity of the *Cloud Queen* were dissipated. With a snort he stalked to the chart rack and entered the fact of his inspection in the log and indorsed it. Then he flung off down the passage, beckoning his two men to follow him.

"Get this stinkpot out of here. I'm through with you," he said as the lock door closed behind him.

"Aye, aye, sir. Thank you, sir." Bullard felt he could afford a little politeness. He was *through*; and in his hand he held a scribbled memorandum of the correct answers to challenges for the next three weeks—the time necessary to reach Ganymede. The Callistan had given him the recognition signals to expedite his trip, so convinced was he that he was dealing with a genuine Venusian.

"Well," said Bullard as he set his jets going again, "that's that. Now all we have to do is straighten out for Oberon, fake a new set of papers, trade this stuff for what we want, and then get back in again."

"That last will be tough, I'm thinking," remarked Red.

"Tough?" was Sparks' contribution. "Damn near impossible, I calls it."

"As long as that 'near' is in we're okay," said Bullard cheerily. "Give 'er another G, Red. We can stand it."

Three times before they cleared the last of the asteroids they were challenged by roving cruisers, but thanks to knowing the answers and also to the general belief that the Earth blockade was break-proof, she was not halted and searched again. Bullard had time to consider his next steps.

The more he pondered the enormous task assigned him, the more he was struck with the irony of the situation. The Earth, mistress of the remnants of what had been the far-flung Tellurian Empire, and a hundredfold more populous and rich than all the other peoples of the Solar System combined, was lying helpless before the might of two of her erstwhile colonies. They lacked the men and the resources to invade the mother planet, but they could, and had, cut her off from all intercourse without. Their strategy was simple. While holding the Tellurian fleet immobile, they would sweep up the remaining Earth colonies—the Saturnian System and what lay beyond. After that they would control the only known supply of the fuel upon which civilization had become dependent. Earth would thereafter have to pay through the nose, for the ultra-powerful Eka-Uranium existed only on Oberon.

This anomalous state of affairs had been made possible by the weak and parsimonious policy followed by the grand council after the successful War of the Rebellion a decade earlier. Having granted the three revolting planets their liberty and signed perpetual treaties of friendship, the Earth allowed its fleet to deteriorate until it was no more than a mere customs patrol. On the other hand, the colonists, embittered by long years of misrule, wanted more than independence—they wanted revenge. Hence they at once began building on a vast scale, but secretly. And when those fleets were strong enough, they struck. Earth, caught utterly unprepared, could not strike back.

They built feverishly, trying to make up for the error of unpreparedness. Every sky yard on the planet worked night and day turning out ships. Soon, every week saw sleek new units, bristling with the most modern armament, making the short jump to Luna, where they were given crews and joined to the fast-growing fleet. In the course of a few months they almost equaled the blockading squadron. A few more months and they would excel it. And then a shocked world learned the awful truth—there was no fuel for such a tremendous fleet. The pacifistic and incapable council had not foreseen this contingency and had provided no reserves. There was only fuel enough for one take-off, and that one necessarily of short duration. What there was must be conserved for emergencies—such as sudden destructive raids on the great Earth cities themselves. Therein lay the delicious irony of the situation. The blockade prevented the arrival of the fuel by which the blockade could easily be broken. Given fuel, the Earth could have all the fuel there was; without it, she must soon capitulate, for it was needed for civil purposes, also. There was already much suffering.

Ship after ship had made the attempt, trying every sort of ruse and trick. None had come back. Bullard had been permitted to make one last try. If he returned within the allotted time, the war would be won; if not, it was to be surrender.

It had been left to him what disguise he would use, and what plan. He chose the simplest one of all—that of a straight merchant ship with no reservations. He had the feeling that the others had been unmasked by their secret armament, and therefore he resolved to carry none. No matter how cleverly concealed, weapons—if adequate— could not escape a really thorough search. The thing must be done by guile, and to that he bent every effort, knowing that success or failure hung on some tiny detail.

Once past the blockading cruisers, he was confronted with the next step—the acquisition of a thousand tons of Eka-Uranium at Oberon. He soon learned, by listening in on the enemy radio, that Oberon had long since fallen and was garrisoned by an expeditionary force from Mars. The *Cloud Queen's* papers would have to be altered to meet another hostile scrutiny, all mention of the fictitious sojourn on Luna must be deleted, and the destination changed. When he had completed his work, the documents purported to show that the ship was straight out of Venus for the outer planets, with cargo unconsigned. Her captain was authorized to trade at discretion and return. He took good care, too, that the page bearing the endorsement of the boarding officer was left in the record. It showed the ship to have been inspected and passed by a control officer.

All went smoothly in Spriteburg. A shipload of Venusian products was most welcome on the desolate planet, and no one raised embarrassing questions. Beyond some haggling as to price and considerable well-simulated indignation at the interplanetary exchange rate quoted, Bullard was called on for little effort. The afternoon of the second day, after he had discharged his cargo, he shot the *Cloud Queen* over the Elfin Range and laid her into the landing docks at the mines. Twenty-four earthly hours after that he was chockablock full of the precious Eka-Uranium. There were a thousand tons of it—enough to fuel the entire new Tellurian fleet to capacity, and with some to spare.

It was not until he called at the captain of the port's office for his clearance papers that he had any premonition of trouble to come. The day of his arrival he had dealt with a deputy, but now it was different. A man sat there whom he had seen before. In a moment he placed him. At the time when he had been in the circumsolar patrol, four years earlier, this captain of the port had been resident on Venus as consul general for Mars. As such he could be expected to be fairly familiar with Venusian shipping. Bullard was thankful for his beard and grayed hairs, for on several occasions he had dined with the man.

The captain of the port signed the papers without a word. As he handed them across the desk to Bullard, he said, in an offhand way:

"I see you are owned by Turnly & Hightower. Please give my regards to Mr. Turnly when you hit Venus again. By the way, how is the old boy? Someone told me he had not been well lately."

"Oh, he keeps going," laughed Bullard, pocketing the papers and the Manual for the Guidance of Neutral Vessels that was handed to him with it. He was affecting a casualness about it that he was far from feeling. In his researches in connection with outfitting the *Cloud Queen*, he had been unable to learn much about her fictitious owners. There was a photo on board showing Mr. Hightower in the front door of the home office, surrounded by the clerical staff, but concerning the senior partner Bullard had been unable to learn anything. It was the weakest link in his armor, and he was ardently hoping the conversation would take another turn.

"So he keeps going," murmured the port captain dreamily, drumming softly on the desk with his plump white fingers. "Hm-m-m. Most uncanny, really." He regarded Bullard thoughtfully for a moment, and then, suddenly, as if aroused from a deep daydream, rose and took his hand. "Well, captain, you may as well take off. Follow the trajectory assigned and you'll have no trouble. A clean

void and a happy landfall to you. And don't forget my
message—Horntrimmer is the name."

As the *Cloud Queen* sped along trajectory XXX-B-37,
dutifully doing all the things required by the Martian-
Jovian rules, Bullard turned this little talk over and over in
his mind. He didn't like it. There was something vaguely
ominous about it. Why uncanny? Horntrimmer's attitude
had been peculiar, to say the least. Yet he had permitted
the ship to clear when it would have been easy to hold her.
If he had been suspicious of her, again why?

Bullard had no answers to these questions, but they
troubled him, nevertheless. He spent his spare hours prowl-
ing the ship or standing in the auxiliary motor room,
studying the equipment. He was racking his brain for a
means to improvise a method of defense if it came to that,
but he found little ground on which to base his hopes.
None, in fact, for the power plant was just sufficient to
operate the ship's legitimate auxiliaries without a dozen
kilowatts to spare. Nor was there an ounce of any sort of
explosive aboard. The ship was truly unarmed. If its disguise failed, all was lost. The only way to break the blockade was to adhere to the plan agreed upon before leaving
Luna.

That plan was daring in its simplicity, and two thirds
of it had been accomplished. There was left only the last
step. Exactly two hundred hours before striking the sphere
of swirling enemy cruisers that constituted the blockade, the
Cloud Queen was to send out a certain signal and keep

repeating it until its receipt was acknowledged. Then she was to climb out of the ecliptic so that she could dive onto Earth from the north, through a region that was thinly patrolled. A few hours before her arrival at the barrier a picked squadron of heavy Tellurian battleships would make a vigorous attack upon a nearby segment of the blockade, using what was left of their hoarded fuel to create a diversion so that the blockade runner could slip through. Cruisers rushing to meet the Tellurian feint would not stop to examine a rusty merchantman, even if they detected her, was the theory. It was upon such a slender thread that the hopes of the Earthmen hung.

It was over the asteroids that Bullard sent his signal, set his deflectors for hard rise, and climbed still higher. And it was but a matter of some eight hours later that the keys of the radio began to clatter out the harsh orders of a pursuing cruiser. The fast Callistan *Folliot* was overhauling the *Cloud Queen* and demanding that she blast down and wait. Bullard's face was drawn and the lines in it hard as he listened to the words being tapped out, but there was nothing to do but comply. He gave the necessary orders.

"As I live and breathe," exclaimed the boarding officer as the inner door of the lock slid open, "if it isn't my old friend, the Venusian! Fancy meeting you here!" It was the identical Callistan who had made the examination on the way out. He oozed sarcasm from every pore. "And—oh, yes, before I forget it—Commodore Horntrimmer instructed me to tell you that Mr. Turnly died three years ago. He was his father-in-law." The Callistan chuckled maliciously. Then he turned to the officer and group of men who had come aboard with him.

"Check these dopes for guns, then set watches. After that you can stow your baggage and settle down. We'll take this bucket in on this course and refuel our own fleet with it." He leered triumphantly at the crestfallen Bullard.

Captain Bullard and his men were not locked up, but forced to carry on their regular duty under the watchful eyes of the prize crew. One or the other of the two officers was always in the control room, sitting in the master's seat at the midst of the main switchboard. Two armed bluejackets stood at the door, ready to carry out any command. The Callistan who had seized the vessel—one Commander Tilsen—produced a fat volume with locked covers and began sending long code messages. The *Folliot*, which had hovered ten or twelve miles on the beam all the while, dashed away, spewing violet fire in her wake. The *Cloud Queen* was left to make the rest of her way alone.

Bullard was forced to stand the same watch as Tilsen took, and had to bear the incessant stream of exultant remarks emanating from him. Although he pretended he had never been fooled in the first place, but had allowed the ship to go on through, knowing full well they could intercept it at will, Bullard knew that he was lying—trying to save face. Tilsen predicted with great relish that as soon as the cargo had been discharged, Bullard would be hustled off to Mars and hanged ignominiously as a spy, together with all his men.

During the first rest period, Bullard lay and tossed and fretted, going over in imagination for the hundredth time every detail of the ship he had come to know well. He must do something, if only warn Earth of the existing state of affairs. But cudgel his brain as he would, he could think of no way to devise a weapon by which he could wrest control from his captors. And then, as he was mentally following the wiring diagram of the vessel for the nth time, a thought struck him as abruptly and as clearly as if a gong had been struck. The infrared projector, of course! There was power—of a sort; five million volts, even if the amperage was trifling. Surely something could be done with that.

That time when the rest period was up he marched to the control room gladly. There were a few details of the ship's construction he had never troubled to note. Now they had taken on a new meaning.

Throughout that watch, his eyes sought the overhead every time he felt the gaze of the sentries off him. He was interested in the exact location of the housing of the searchlight perched on the hull above. It was clearly delineated by the double row of rivets, the center being almost directly over the seat whereon the Callistan Tilsen sat, talking glibly of the tortures the Martian code permitted on certain types of condemned prisoners. Bullard yawned as he pretended to listen, his mind busy with multiplying and adding the estimated distance between groups of rivets. Before the watch was over he knew what he wanted to know, and spent the remainder of the time memorizing the facts he had observed.

That rest period he did not toss and fret. He knew precisely what he wanted to do. Fifteen minutes after the watch below had settled to its rest, Bullard was scudding down the darkened passage, bound for the engineer's storeroom. Except for the guards in the control room, and one in the auxiliary generator room, the ship was unpatrolled. The captors were contemptuous of their victims, serene in the belief that there was nothing they could do.

Bullard shut the door of the storeroom behind him. A moment later he was hard at work with a hacksaw, cutting off a six-foot length of one-inch round copper bar taken from the electrical stock. And when he had done that he seized a file and beveled one end of it to as nearly forty-five degrees as he could make it. It was but a matter of minutes before he was done, for the metal was not hard.

Up to that point he was well satisfied, but when he went to get a heavy-metal disk he found that what he wanted was not in store. He took down a tube hand-hole plug and examined it critically. It was of platinum, four inches in diameter, but much too thick—it would not do. For fifteen minutes he pawed through the bins, but all the disk-shaped pieces were too wide or not wide enough, or of light metals such as steel and bronze. A high atomic number he *must* have.

Just as a fresh wave of discouragement swept over him, he thought of the handful of 100-uran pieces he had taken in Oberon to adjust the differences of the values of the cargoes he had traded. Those massive three-inch coins were minted of gold, alloyed with a little iridium. For shape, size and composition they were exactly what he needed. Before the watch was over he had brazed one neatly to the beveled end of his long copper rod, and the face of the tilted disk shone like a mirror where he had filed it smooth. He stood it in a corner, along with the tube scrapers, and went back to his bunk, well pleased with his first step.

The seemingly interminable tour of duty came to an end. Bullard counted the seconds, after they had been relieved, so anxious was he to get on with the task he had set himself. At the end of ten minutes all appeared to be quiet, so he stole away to the storeroom. His odd-shaped rod was still there, unmolested. He took a space helmet from the rack and put it on. He slung the brazing kit over his shoulder, picked up a sledge, a pair of wrenches, and the gold-tipped copper rod and made his way to the space lock.

No one heard him go out, for he eased the doors very carefully to, and the hull was so well insulated that once he was outside the slight noise caused by his scuffing shoes could not be heard within. He crawled straight for the head-light and stacked his tools beside it. One by one he backed off the nuts that held the focusing lens to its frame. Then he lifted it out and went to work on the filters behind it. At the end of the half-hour he had come to the front end of the vacuum tube itself, which he broke with one hard lick of the sledge. It was a trying and dirty job to pry the complicated heating elements out, and he had to watch out for the fragments of the tube, but within another hour he had the tube clean of all it had formerly held. He lay full length in a hollow cylinder, ten feet long by a yard in diameter. Near each end of it were the cable terminals, waiting to be tapped.

Swiftly he erected the rod on the base formed by the inner end, and brazed it into place. Then he hooked it up to the cable end. He had formed the cathode of his contrivance. He backed away to the open end of the housing, and there he rigged an anode. When he was done he replaced the outermost piece he had removed to get in, bolted it fast, then went below. His watch showed he had an hour to spare. He had plenty of time to whisper a few words of instruction to Sparks, under whose desk the foot switch that operated the headlight was located.

When they went on watch again, Sparks kicked the switch shut, and Bullard took up his surreptitious vigil. He knew it would take time, but he did not know how much. He knew there were going to be some extraordinary results, but he did not know quite what. But three hundred milliamperes flung at a golden disk at five million volts' pressure was sure to do something.

The watch wore on, with Tilsen's customary string of jibes. At the end of the first hour the Callistan's flow of words began to jerk to a stop more frequently, and the pauses between bursts became longer. The man began to wear a puzzled, hurt expression, and several times he took off his cap and rubbed his head. He did not seem to notice that hair by the handful showered down upon his shoulders after the last such head caressing.

"What the hell has gone wrong with the air?" he screamed suddenly, springing up from his seat and then settling back into it. "Oh, how my head aches!"

Red Leary checked the indicators and sang out their readings. Everything was normal; the air-conditioning system was functioning perfectly. The big Callistan scowled at him, not acknowledging, but apparently accepting what Red said. He resumed his former position, but would stoop ever so often to snatch at his leg. Presently he called to one of the Callistan sailors who stood on guard at the back of the room. When the sailor came up to him he leaned forward and plucked some imaginary something away from his thigh.

"Take that damn thing out and kill it," he directed, his voice full of venom. "Blasted wildcat!"

After that he slumped a little in the saddle and dropped his chin on his chest, brooding. Bullard measured his posture carefully by eye and wondered whether the tilt of his head had thrown him out of the cone of invisible rays that was playing down from above. But apparently it had not, for at the end of another quarter hour Tilsen sprang suddenly erect, his eyes almost starting from his head.

"Back! Back! Back 'er full! Glaciers ahead!" He was shrieking wildly and clawing at the board in front of him. A trembling hand came to rest on a glazed clock face, and the smooth crystal seemed to soothe him. He ceased yelling and sat shuddering as he was, with beads of cold sweat rolling off his brow and splashing down onto the board. One of his ears twitched violently, fluttering like a leaf in the breeze. The two bluejackets had come up closer and were watching him in alarm, wide-eyed.

"Shall I call your relief, sir?" asked one of them timidly.

Tilsen was a hard man, even with his own. He swung in the chair, staring coldly and malignantly at the man. "So serpents speak in this valley?" he hissed, sliding out of his chair into a half crouch, as if about to spring at the unfortunate man. His hand went to the butt of his ray gun as the terrified sailor backed away from him. Like lightning, he drew and went into frenzied action. He cut down the first sailor with a blast that seared away half his chest, and before the other could bring himself to fire on his own officer, him, too, he blasted. Then, with a mighty curse, he flung his gun at the bodies and stood swaying drunkenly where he stood.

Bullard looked on with awe, wondering what his handiwork would bring next.

Just as the other officer appeared in the doorway with the remaining sailors crowded behind, Tilsen seemed to lose all interest in his surroundings. He began picking at himself, slowly at first, as if to rid himself of imaginary ants, and then more wildly, until in another minute he was tearing at his clothes as if they were on fire. Then he gave one ear-splitting scream and fell to the deck in convulsions, rolling, kicking and biting. It was there that his fellow countrymen overpowered him and slipped the irons about his wrists and ankles.

"What did you do to him?" demanded the officer of Bullard furiously.

Bullard shrugged. "He went mad—that is all. How could I help that?"

The officer gazed at the helpless, writhing form at his feet. Not the most casual glance could miss noticing the horrible condition of the head. Not only had the hair been stripped away from top and back, but the skin and the superficial flesh as well. It was as if a mysterious flame had seared it. Yet no known weapon made such a wound— a blaster would have burned the whole skull away.

He examined the room intently, and even went so far as to expose plates set at various angles about the master's chair, but Sparks had kicked his switch open long before— at the moment the crazed Callistan had sprung from the seat. The developed plates showed nothing.

"That's damned funny," muttered the Callistan lieutenant as he studied them. "It *must* have been hard radiation —nothing else could have made those brands."

He frowned and tossed the featureless plates into a corner. Maybe his commander was just a bit crazy, after all, he told himself. There had been occasions—

"I'll take over," he barked, glowering at the watching Earthmen.

Then he slid into the master's seat himself.

"That's the story," finished Bullard three days later.

"We did the same thing to his sidekick. After that the men were easy. We brought in two alive."

He was standing before the desk of the admiral commandant of Luna base. Outside, safely nestled in the vast crater, the battered *Cloud Queen* lay, a huge battleship alongside either side taking on the vital fuel.

"Thanks to the battle you put on, as per schedule, there was only one enemy cruiser in our way, and we fooled him into letting us pass. We had the Martian code book, you know. We sent him a tripled triple-x, which in their code signifies, 'On urgent confidential mission of highest importance; do not interfere.' "

"Nice work," congratulated the admiral. "I'll see that you get the Celestial Cross and a promotion at the very least. But how—"

"Gamma rays," said Bullard. "I knew they played hell with living organism, so the only problem I had was to rig up a giant x-ray machine where I could bring it to bear on those birds, knowing that they would not suspect until it was too late. You can't feel the things, you know.

"For that I needed a huge vacuum tube, a cathode of the right material, and scads of voltage. By going outside the hull I had my vacuum readymade; the cathode I improvised out of stuff on board; the voltage was already there, awaiting the flip of a switch. The fact that the gamma rays had to go through an inch of iridium steel didn't detract much from their poisonous qualities. In fact, I imagine the secondary radiations from the radiated iron did almost as much damage as the hard stuff bouncing off that gold 100-

uran piece. Anyhow, it was enough to addle their brains. By the time their reaction was strong enough to tip them off that something was wrong, they were too far gone to be able to add two and two and get anything out of it."

"Sort of homemade Coolidge tube, eh?" observed the admiral commandant.

"Sort of," grinned Bullard, thinking of the unholy mess he had made of a perfectly good Venusian infrared searchlight. "But it worked."

WHEN *all the odds are stacked against a man, then he uses his courage and wit to the last ounce, to the finish of himself or the enemy. Captain Bullard had lost the war on a barren asteroid—the enemy were very sure of that. Only they had not been able to convince him—and with a little reflection and ingenuity Bullard was able to make the final engagement a memorable one.*

BULLARD REFLECTS

· "Whee! Yippee! Yow!"

The crowd went crazy. Staid, gold-braided captains and commanders jumped up and down on their seats and yelled themselves hoarse. Even the admirals present dropped their dignified hand clapping for unrestrained shouting. Space-men of all ratings tossed their hats away, hugged whoever was next to them, and behaved generally like wild men. Alan MacKay had scored his tenth successive goal!

"Castor Beans, Castor Beans—waw! waw! waw!" went the *Pollux* bleachers derisively.

"Polliwogs, Polliwogs—yah, yah, yah!" came the prompt response from the space cruiser *Castor's* side of the arena. But it was a weak and disheartened chorus. Eight hundred and fifty to twenty-five the wrong way at the end

127

of the first half was not the sort of score to inspire a cheering section. The *Pollux's* Dazzle Dart team was mopping up—and how!

Captain Bullard of the *Pollux* was no exception to the rest. He flopped back into his seat red of face and utterly exhausted. His vocal cords had gone long since, and now he could only gasp and speak in weak whispers. Captain Ellington, commander of the mine division, leaned over and congratulated him.

"You've got the General Excellence Trophy in the bag," he said. "That is the third time in a row, isn't it? That means you keep it."

"Yes," said Bullard feebly. "But, oh, boy, who would have dreamed of picking up a player like this MacKay! I asked for him on account of the way he handled that Jovian surrender, but I had no idea he was such a whiz at Dazzle Dart—"

Then Bullard's husky voice failed him altogether, and he turned to watch the parades between halves.

The interfleet athletic meet, held for the first time since the Jovian armistice, had been a howling success from his point of view from first to last. The hand-picked, well-trained skymen of the *Pollux* had taken every major sport. The meteor-ball contest had been a pushover; they earned over eight hundred of the possible thousand points at saltation—that grueling competition of leaping from a stand at all gravities from zero to two and a half. They had outswum, outrun and outplayed their competitors in practically every one of the events. And now, in the most critical test of all, they had a walkaway. He had expected it, of course, but not by such a tremendous margin.

In the meantime the crowd milled and whooped on the plain at the bottom of Luna's well-dome crater Ashtaroth which was the athletic field of the great Lunar Base. Captain Bullard regained his breath and sat watching. Good boys, his, he was thinking, all of them—whether at war or at play. Then there came another touch at his elbow and Lieutenant Commander Bissel was there, aid to the commandant.

"I hate to inject a serious note into the festivities," he apologized, "but there's something hot coming in over the transether. Remember Egon Ziffler, chief of secret police of the Jovian Empire—the Torturer, they called him?"

Bullard nodded.

"He's been located, and at Titania, of all places. He appeared in a Callistan cruiser and took the place by surprise. Apparently he massacred the entire garrison in the most fiendish manner; the admiral is talking now with the sole survivor who, somehow, managed to escape to Oberon. The worst of it is he is in possession of our experimental arsenal and proving grounds—"

"Yes?" said Bullard.

"Yes. It has not been released yet, but that deadly new electron gun worked perfectly and there are hundreds of them there. With those in their hands they will be almost invulnerable. Only the screens of a Star-class cruiser can resist the handsize model, and I doubt if those could stand up to the heavier Mark II we planned to build."

"That's bad," remarked Bullard, with a sigh. It seemed that no matter how much cleanup work they did, there was always trouble.

"Yes," agreed Bissel soberly, "it is bad. But I'll toddle along and get the latest. By the time this is over maybe I can give you the full dope."

He slid out of the box, and Bullard turned his attention once more to the field, only now his thoughts were inside the *Pollux*, parked in her launching rack over at the sky yard. Swiftly he surveyed mentally every compartment in her, then he permitted himself to relax. He could find no fault. She was ready to soar. Just let them give the word.

By that time the playing field was empty. A whistle blew. The second half was about to begin. It seemed a useless waste of time, but the rules were unchangeable. A fleet championship game could not be conceded; it must be played out to the last second.

The Castoreans came onto the field in a somewhat more cheerful frame of mind. In this half they would have the advantage. They had the offensive. Then the Polliwogs tramped in, still jubilant. There was an enormous margin to their credit. They could hardly lose.

The game, essentially, was a simple one. But it called for the utmost a man could develop in alertness, agility and dexterity. Moreover, to get the best results, there must be instant teamwork, secured by long practice, for there was scant time to interpret and act upon the sharply barked code signals that demanded various degrees of cooperation.

The elements of it were these: it was played on a court not much different in layout from that required by basketball, football, or jai-alai. There were two opposite goals, set high in backstops. The goals were six-inch black holes in which were selenium units. A semicircular wall, four feet high, guarded a forbidden area at the foot of each backstop. The quarterback of the offensive team had a flashlight—a superflashlight—which was loaded for each half with exactly one hundred ten-second flashes of light. The light was delivered in a thin pencil of one centimeter in diameter, and the inner mechanism of it was so designed that the operator could deliver one flash at a time by simply pointing it and pressing a button. But once the button was pressed, the light stayed on for a full ten seconds and then went out abruptly, counting as one serve. The idea was to cast the ray into the opposite goal hole. If the bell rang, the quarterback scored twenty-five points.

The defenders' aim was to intercept and deflect the light —into the other goal, if possible. Should they succeed, their score would be double. To effect this, they were equipped with as many slightly convex mirrors as they thought they could handle. The mirrors were not dissimilar from the type worn on the brow of a throat specialist. Players usually wore them strapped to their wrists, but stars could not only manage those, but also ones strapped at their waists and on the head as well. A good jumper

was a distinct asset to a team, and the *Pollux's* five saluta-
tory champs had been of invaluable assistance.

They took their positions. Weems, captain of the *Castor*
team, had the torch. His twenty guards were ranged about
him. The Polliwogs scattered out at the other end of the
court, tense and waiting. Tackling, holding or slugging
was barred, but a man could drop on all fours and make an
onrushing opponent stumble over him. There was no more
to the game than that.

Weems maneuvered for position, then leaped unex-
pectedly into the air, and it was a goodly leap, as they
were playing on strictly Lunar gravity. At near the top of
his flight his hand darted forth and he sent a beam of light
at his goal. It struck the backstop not a foot from the goal,
but before the eagle-eyed Weems could shift his hand, a
Polliwog player was in the air and had caught it with one
of his reflectors. A twist of the wrist sent it hurtling back
to the other side, a narrow miss. The source of it—Weems
—was falling now, and he jerked his arm, throwing the
light sharply downward, where one of his own teammates
caught it and shot it up at a steep angle under the hovering
Polliwog guards. A bull's-eye! And not an instant too soon,
for at that moment the light went out. Twenty-five points
for the attackers.

So it went—so swiftly the eye could hardly follow.
Despite the fact that it was customary to fill the arena dome
with humid air and spray dust in it so as to illuminate the
darting beam throughout its length, it took the glance of an
eagle to keep pace with it. A battery of cameras, of course,

recorded the play constantly, and the selenium-cell-operated bell bonged from time to time as the light ray hit it.

The second half was full of brilliant double and triple plays, where often the quarterback would turn and flash his light directly behind him to a confederate who relayed it across the court, who in his turn shot it into a momentarily undefended goal. The ultimate score, though, was against the Castoreans. Their defeat was so decisive as to admit no quibbling.

The cheering lasted for minutes, but hardly had the final goal bell rung before Bullard was aware that the grand admiral himself had entered his box and was sitting beside him.

"Congratulations," said he, then addressed himself to serious business. "You have already heard a little of what is going on on Titania? I sent Bissel. It is a scurvy trick to recall your crew and send you out on a desperate mission at an hour like this, but there is no other ship ready. Since the armistice it seems that there has been a letdown in discipline. Can you blast off in four hours?"

"I can blast off in one hour if you'll give me an all-Moon hookup on the public-address system," said Bullard, without batting an eye. He had not only been expecting the detail, but hoping for it. Ziffler was a creature he loathed from the bottom of his heart—treacherous, cruel, and unprincipled, of a breed that extermination is the only cure for.

Within five minutes Bullard was making his appeal to his skymen.

"On the double!" were his last words, and he slammed down the transmitter.

The burned and looted fortress of Caliban lay directly under. Bullard pushed his navigator aside and took the controls himself. He set the antigravs at half strength and slowly lost altitude, constantly searching. At last he found them. There was a parked cruiser of the *Dernfug* class, and a horde of men camped outside alongside it. Phosphorescent flares burned, and he saw they were celebrating. Kegs of the type used as containers for the potent *snahger* liquor rolled all about, and the thickest of the rioting throng were gathered about others yet upright.

"The ship, first," said Bullard, grimly, and his gunnery officer—Fraser—said only, "Aye, aye, sir."

The searing, blinding beam of incredible power leaped downward, played a moment on the cruiser, then flickered out. On the ground there was left only a mass of running molten metal, sputtering a valedictory of brilliant sparks.

"Cease firing!" was Bullard's next crisp order. "The grand admiral wants them brought in alive, if possible." He reached for the antigrav control and pushed the deflectors on hard swing.

The *Pollux* came down a mile away to an easy landing on the dark plain. The people in her could plainly see the floodlamps of the rollicking bandits and the sharp reflections that glinted on the smooth terrain between. There was nothing to impede the progress of the landing force.

But by the time the landing force was ready for its trip,

the lookout reported a new development. A party of men was approaching, and they were stretching their arms over their heads in gesture of surrender. A close scrutiny of them could discover no arms worth worrying about. The new electron projectors were said to be quite heavy, each requiring two men to carry and operate. Any less potent weapon the veterans of the *Pollux* could deal with, and deal with well.

"Find out who they are and what is their proposition," ordered Bullard. "If it sounds reasonable, let three in for a parley. No more. He is full of slimy tricks, that Ziffler. I wouldn't trust his words under any circumstances."

It was not Ziffler, but Skul Drosno, former vice premier of the Jovian regime, together with two high aids. They wanted to arrange terms of surrender, they said. Their story was that they had revolted against the atrocities of Ziffler and had him a prisoner in their camp. They would trade him—trussed up as he was—for personal immunity and a general pardon for their followers. They would willingly submit to trial, knowing now how they had been hoodwinked.

"Let them in," said Bullard though he was still a trifle doubtful. "I will talk with them."

Skul Drosno began his appeal. Bullard recognized it at once as rank sophistry, but he continued to listen. Then, to his astonishment, Drosno suddenly slumped in his chair. His eyes were crossed to a painful degree, and his hands wavered uncertainly in the air. The next moment he pitched forward onto the deck and sprawled, apparently unconscious. One of his aids looked sick, and staggered to his feet, weaving about ridiculously.

"What an act!" thought Bullard, and sprang to his own feet, alert. He shot a glance to his side and saw that his executive, Moore, who had been with him, was an inert heap. And at that moment things began to blur before his own eyes. His knees wobbled, and he heard a harsh, metallic ringing in his ears. He fought for air, then choked. The floor plates rushed upward and struck him squarely in the face. After that Bullard remembered no more.

The next voice he heard was the high-pitched cackling of the unspeakable Ziffler.

"Can such things be!" crowed the vile Callistan. "A great personage, no less. I find as my prisoner the inimitable, the invincible, the incorruptible Bullard—hero of the nine planets!"

Bullard opened his eyes, ignoring the pounding in the back of his head. He was seated in a chair, strapped hand and foot, and the swaggering ex-police chief who had terrorized the Jovian satellites was standing before him, exulting.

"Perhaps he is not so invincible," pursued his tormentor, calmly lighting a cigarette and seating himself. "We have never seen him outside his formidable *Pollux*. But now that he is in our hands, I am curious to see how good he is. Hagstund! Come here!"

A big brute of a former convict strode forward.

"What do you say? Shall we have a little sport? Why not put these men in spacesuits and turn them loose for twenty-four hours? Then we can have a hunt. This man, in particular, has a gr-r-reat reputation for cleverness. Let's see what he can do on a barren and resourceless planet. We have counted them, so we know their numbers. I will give a prize, prizes. Ten thousand sols for this one, to whoever brings him down. Another ten thousand for the last man of the lot and another five for the next to the last. It'll be good fun, eh?"

Ziffler took a swig of *snahger* and delivered himself of an elaborate wink. Bullard did not believe for a moment he was drunk. Ziffler was too clever a scoundrel for that. It was a gesture meant to raise false hopes. Bullard knew all too well what the wastes of Titania were. He had been there before. Except for the port of Caliban, the arsenal and a few scattered stations which no doubt had been plundered by now, there was nothing but bleak, frozen plains, broken by rugged meteor craters.

"Swell, chief," agreed the henchman. "What about the ship?"

"Leave her lie as she is. They'll not send another for days. I don't want you baboons monkeying around inside her. Let's give these guys a run, then we'll get down to business. There's plenty of time."

Rough hands pulled Bullard to his feet, and at the point of one of the new and deadly electron guns they made him put on an ordinary spacesuit. As the mists cleared away in his throbbing head, he saw that he was in a large hall, and that other men and officers of his crew were being similarly treated.

"Oh, by the way," remarked Ziffler offhandedly. "They say I am unkind. I'll save you one bit of mental torture. What got you down was our new hypnotic dust. It's very clever, really. Powder a coat with it, for example, then expose it to air. It vaporizes and puts everyone to sleep. My emissaries went out, too—naturally. All but one, that is, who had been heavily doped with an antidote before-hand. He survived long enough to open the door for us, then, unfortunately, died. It was regrettable, but in my business I find it necessary to do such things."

Bullard said not a word. He was ready. The outlook was black, but he had seen other outlooks that were quite as black.

"I'll be seeing you, Ziffler," he said, and hoped it was not mere braggadocio. Ziffler had a reputation for sadism, but not for courage. There was the bare chance that that single psychological shot in the dark might in time be digested and unsettle him. "Let's go. I prefer anything to your presence."

"Yeah?" said Ziffler, but he beckoned to his strong-arm squad.

The entire crew of the *Pollux* was there. They were pushed out through the portal of the dome in squads of four and told to get going. Bullard was let out last of all. Their captors promised tauntingly that they had a full Earth day before pursuit.

"Stay together, men," called Bullard into his helmet microphone, the moment the portal closed behind him. "All officers come up close to me."

The light on Titania is dim, even in full daytime. But it was good enough for his officers to read the swift manipulations of his fingers. Their skipper was using the sign language all trained Space Guard men used when they feared their words might be overheard.

"Poleward from here," Bullard told them, "some thirty miles, is a meteorite crater. For several years we have maintained a secret laboratory there and it is possible that these ruffians have not discovered it. That will be our destination. Under this gravity we should reach it within a few hours, though I am uncertain of its exact direction. Have the men spread out and hunt. There should be flares there, and the first man in should light one. The last time I visited the place it had a staff of eight or ten scientists, and an excellent interplanetary radio. They may have weapons, but at least we can flash an alarm."

Rapidly waved arms acknowledged, and the Polliwogs dispersed in the semidarkness.

It was Lieutenant Alan MacKay who reached the spot first. He had trouble in finding a flare, but eventually he found one and lit it. The laboratory was a shambles. The vandals had found the place, despite his captain's hopes to the contrary, and turned it upside down. The bodies of the physicists and chemists lay all about, among them that of the unhappy director. Torn papers, broken glass and tangled wire littered the floor. The radio had been smashed almost out of recognition. MacKay, a newcomer to the service, shuddered, but he carried out his orders.

Bullard arrived shortly after, and his face was not pretty to see as he viewed the wreckage. Now he regretted the flare. *They* undoubtedly had seen it too. He had hoped to warn these people, send a message to the System in general, then have his forces scatter. A few of them might have hoped to survive the ruthless man hunt that was to follow.

But the situation was changed, and since any alternative seemed as hopeless as any other, he let the flare continue to burn. By keeping together, some resistance might be improvised. While he was waiting for the stragglers to come up, he busied himself with reassembling the torn pages of the notebooks and journals strewn about the floor.

Much of them dealt with routine analysis, but on a page written in red ink and numbered "97" he found a fragment that brought him to eager attention.

Unlike most meteorites, the one that made this crater failed to disintegrate upon impact—or rather, not all of it disintegrated. We have discovered a number of fragments, slightly curved, that indicate it was stratified, and that the stratum of radius, of about thirty meters and of one and a fraction inches in thickness, simply broke into bits instead of molecules. In the storehouse in the crater bottom there are more than a hundred of these fragments, running up to as high as twenty centimeters across. They are of a jade-like substance, subject to abrasion by ordinary methods and can be drilled by steel drills, and are not hard and ultradense as might have been expected. The curious thing about these fragments is that they defy x-ray analysis. For some odd reason they wreck every tube that is brought to bear upon them. They backfire, so to speak. Can it be that—

The page was at an end. Bullard sought frantically for page 98, but he could not find it. He called the trusty Benton.

"Take a gang of men and go down and search the crater. You ought to find a storehouse and in it a bunch of junky-looking rock fragments that look like jade. If you do, bring a flock of them up here. Quick!"

To the others standing around, he said:

"Clear out the wreckage in the workshop and see if those breast drills can be made to work. Strip the boots off of those dead men and cut them up into straps. As soon as you have done that, take off your own and cut them up, too. We haven't got time to lose."

Presently Lieutenant Benton came back, and a number of men were with him. They all bore armfuls of slightly curved pieces of a moss-colored, glasslike substance. Each was fairly large, but all had irregular and jagged edges. Bullard examined one hurriedly, hefting it critically.

"Get MacKay up here—quickly," he barked, suddenly. Then he wheeled on Benton. "Take all of these and drill two pairs of holes through each—here and here"—and he showed him. "Then affix straps, just as you would to those mirrors you use in the Dazzle Dart game."

Benton looked at him wonderingly, but he had learned a long time before to put his trust in his remarkable commander. He piled the shiny fragments of meteor stuff together and went out to call in his men.

Bullard felt better. What he was about to attempt was a wild gamble, but it was immeasurably better than waiting like a sheep for the slaughter or fleeing hopelessly across the cold wastes of Titania. He was very thankful, too, that on the occasion of his last visit to that satellite he had cut the governor general's party and ball and visited this secluded laboratory instead. For the day he had been there was shortly after the experiments described on the isolated page he now held in his hand. At that time nothing had been definitely determined as to the structure of the mysterious crystalline substance salvaged from the crater, but he recalled the speculations of the now dead scientists concerning it.

Lieutenant MacKay reported.

"Yes, sir?"

"Tell Commander Moore to have all the members of the Dazzle Dart team report to you here at once, and that means the men on the second team and the scrubs as well. Tell him to have everyone else find pits in the crater bottom and take shelter there until further orders. Clear?"

The ruffians of the Ziffler gang did not play entirely fair, as was to be expected. They beat the gun by several hours. It was Benton, in charge of the lookout, who sighted the mob advancing across the plain. They were in fairly close formation, as if by direction finders or some other means they already knew that the *Pollux* men were not scattered, but together at the so-called "Mystery Crater."

"Take stations," ordered Bullard, crisply. He was standing in the semidarkness on the crater rim, some distance away from the damaged laboratory. To the right and left of him his victorious Dazzle Dart team were lying behind the irregular parapet made by the crater wall.

"Benton!" he called. "Scatter your squad both ways from me. When that gang of hoodlums is halfway up the hill, let 'em have your flame-gun blast. Then duck and beat it for the bottom of the crater and hide out until I call 'all clear.' "

Benton had found eight old flame guns in a work shed. They had been obsolete as fighting weapons for many years, but could deliver a nasty burn.

Captain Bullard had another look at the advancing hunting party. He saw that they had brought along a number of the new electron guns and were beginning to struggle up to the talus with them. The yelling mob reached a sort of ledge and waited for the guns to be brought up. A jeering voice, louder than the rest, called up:

"Will you come down and take it, you lice, or do we have to come up there and get you?"

"Now!" said Bullard softly into his microphone.

Eight feeble heat machines spat their ruddy blasts, then went out with a jerk as their operators let go of them and

slid down the inner wall to safety. It was well that Bullard
had foreseen the reply they would get, for the counterblast
came almost instantaneously. A score of bright stars flamed
out downhill and from them thin streams of almost invisible
violet fire lashed upward and played along the crater
rim. The rock sprang into incandescence and inches of it
melted and flowed as bubbling, sparkling slag down the
slope, where it quickly dulled to red and congealed.

"Now?" asked MacKay anxiously. He was crouched beside the skipper.

"Not yet. Wait until they are closer."

The assault went on for a moment, then stopped. Bullard
took a cautious peep and saw the Callistans had resumed
their climb.

"What's the dirtiest thing you can call a Callistan?"
whispered Bullard, grinning unseen in the dark. "You
know the lingo."

"*Froahbortlen,*" replied MacKay without hesitation.
The Callistan language was rich in epithets, but that one
was the most comprehensive and unequivocal ever coined
in any language. Even a depraved criminal of the lowest
grade would resent it.

"Invite them up," said Bullard, grimly. "When they
answer, do your stuff."

"On your toes, men," MacKay warned his teammates.
Then he opened his mike wide and issued his sizzling,
triple-barreled, insulting invitation.

Bullard involuntarily caught his breath. The die was
cast. For an instant one of the qualms of uncertainty that

rarely came to him held him in its grip. Was he right, or would they fail? Which side would be the victims of the massacre about to begin? Well, in a couple of seconds he would know.

The properties of the strange meteor substance were still unknown. It stopped Gamma and other hard rays. It wrecked the x-ray tubes focused upon it. How could that be, unless it also possessed that long-hunted, but never found, property of being able to deflect and reflect the high-pressure beams?

MacKay's helmet still vibrated with the last vile words of his superb taunt when the answering salvo of electric fire came. But that time there was more than inert rock to receive it. A row of alert young men stood on the crest, and a weird-looking crew they were. Glistening bits of rock were strapped to their wrists, to their foreheads, their belts, and even their ankles. In an instant they were leaping, dancing and twisting like mad dervishes, deftly parrying every violet pencil that struck above the rock at their feet. The devastating power was being hurled back whence it came.

The ruffians must have been amazed at the swift return of fire from men they thought to be totally disarmed, but they hung on doggedly for a few seconds more. Then their fire ceased altogether, and all that the observers on the rim could see were a few scared survivors scrambling down the way they had come.

"Too bad we haven't a weapon," sighed Bullard. "We could make a clean sweep."

He whipped out a flashlight and strode down to the ledge. There were many of the abandoned electron guns standing about on tripods, or overturned by the fleeing gangsters. Something soft gave under Bullard's boot. He played his light along the ground and saw a sight that under other circumstances would have been revolting. Loose hands and feet, attached to charred stumps of arm or leg, were strewn widely. Other and less readily identifiable fragments of disintegrated humanity lay among them. Ziffler's strong-arm squad, once the terror of the outer planets, had been dispersed in the fullest sense of the word.

Bullard turned on his amplifier.

"Okay, Moore. Round up the men and bring them down. We're going back."

The trek back across the icy waste seemed infinitely shorter and easier than it had on the outward journey. Men's hearts were light now, and not leaden as before. To the Polliwogs, the knowledge they had lost their ship had been as dispiriting as the seeming certainty of their impeding doom. Now all that was changed. A mile ahead of them lay the *Pollux*, just as they had left her.

The search for Ziffler and the stragglers took some time, but they found them, cowering and whimpering behind a boulder.

"Iron them well and throw them into the brig," snapped Bullard, and went into his ship.

He grabbed a signal pad and wrote a brief report.

A little later the grand admiral at Lunar Base stretched

out his hand for the flimsy bit of yellow paper his orderly had brought him. He read it, then read it again. He frowned a little and scratched his head.

"Has Bullard gone highbrow on us?" he asked, tossing the message over to Bissel. Bissel picked it up and read:

After reflection, the enemy succumbed.

BULLARD.

*To the victors belong the spoils, or they should at least
be rewarded with a period of rest and refreshment. But
this time the problem was to retain their rightful share.*

*Homeward bound, with pay and bonus money burning in
their pockets and shore (or planet) leave ahead, Captain
Bullard and his crew came up against a totally new peril—
the wiles of a civilian politician. And they might have
lost everything had not Bullard produced a last-minute
ace, in the person of Brimstone Bill.*

BRIMSTONE BILL

·The prisoners were herded into the room and ranged
against one of the bulkheads. Captain Bullard sat stiffly
behind his desk regarding the group of ruffians with a gaze
of steely appraisal. Lieutenant Benton and a pair of
pistoled bluejackets were handling the prisoners, while
Commander Moore stood at the back of Bullard's desk,
looking on. Then Bullard gave a jerk of his head and the
procession started. One by one they shuffled to the spot
before his desk, clanking their heavy chains at each
dragging step. And one by one the captain of the *Pollux*
surveyed them, critically and coldly, comparing their appearance and their marks with the coded descriptions in the
ethergram on his desk.

149

These were the survivors of the notorious Ziffler gang, captured on Oberon the month before, after the encounter on the lip of a little crater that the Polliwogs had already come to call the "Battle of the Mirrors." The first, of course, was Egon Ziffler himself, all his arrogance and bluster melted away long since. Then came Skul Drosno, his chief aid, and there followed ten other plug-uglies who had survived the holocaust of reflected fire. All were big hulking brutes of Callistans, ray-blackened, scarred, and hairy. The last and thirteenth man was of a different type altogether. Bullard waited in silence until he had ranged himself before his desk.

"Paul Grogan," called Benton, checking the final name on the list.

"Hm-m-m," said Bullard, looking at the miserable specimen standing at a grotesque version of "attention" before him, and then glancing at the Bureau of Justice's ethergram summary of his pedigree. After that he studied the prisoner in detail. He was a queer fish indeed to have been caught in such a haul.

The self-styled Grogan was a wizened, underfed little fellow and bore himself with an astonishing blend of cringing and swagger. The strangest thing about him was his head, which was oversize for his body. He had a fine forehead topped with a leonine mane of iron-gray hair, which after a cursory glance might have been called a noble head. But there was an occasional shifty flicker of the eyes and a twitching at the mouth that belied that judgment. Bullard referred to the Bureau's memo again.

"Grogan," it said, "probably Zander, alias Ardwell, alias Nordham, and many other names. Small-time crook and chiseler, card sharp, confidence man. Arrested often throughout Federation for petty embezzlement, but no convictions. Not known to have connection with Ziffler gang."

"Hm-m-m," said Bullard again. He had placed Grogan, et cetera, now in his memory. It had been a long time since the paths of the two had crossed, but Bullard never forgot things that happened to him. Nor did he see fit to recall it too distinctly to his prisoner, for he was not altogether proud of the recollection. But to check his own powers of retention, he asked:

"You operated on Venus at one time—as an itinerant preacher, if the record is correct—under the name of Brimstone Bill?"

"Why, yes, sir, now that you mention it," admitted Brimstone Bill, with a sheepish grin. "But, oh, sir, I quit that long ago. It didn't pay."

"Really?" remarked Bullard. That was not his recollection of it. He had visited Venus in those days as a Passed Midshipman. One night, in the outskirts of Erosburg, they had curiously followed a group of skymen into a lighted hall emblazoned with the sign, "Come, See and Hear BRIMSTONE BILL—Free Admittance." And they went, saw and heard. That bit of investigation had cost the youthful Bullard just a month's pay—all he had with him. For he had fallen under the spell of the fiery oratory of the little man with the big bushy head and flashing eyes, and after groveling before the rostrum and confessing himself a wicked boy, he had turned his pockets wrongside out to find some worthy contribution to further "the cause." Bullard winced whenever he thought of it.

"No, sir, it didn't pay," said the little man. "In money, yes. But not in other ways."

"The police, eh?"

"Oh, not at all, sir," protested Brimstone Bill. "Everything I ever did was strictly legal. It was the suckers . . . uh, the congregation, that is. They got wise to me. A smart-aleck scientist from the gormel mills showed me up one night—"

He lifted his manacled hands and turned them so the palms showed outward. Deep in each palm was a bright-red, star-shaped scar.

"They crucified me. When the police cut me down the next day, I swore I'd never preach again. And I won't, so help me."

"You are right about that," said Bullard grimly, satisfied that his memory was as good as he thought it was. "This last time you have stretched your idea of what's legal beyond its elastic limit. The gang you were caught with is on its way to execution."

Brimstone Bill emitted a howl and fell to his knees, whining and pleading.

"Save that for your trial," said Bullard harshly. "Take 'em away, Benton."

After they had all gone, Bullard sat back and relaxed. He promptly dismissed Ziffler and his mob from his mind.

The Oberon incident was now a closed book. It was one more entry in the glorious log of the *Pollux*. It was the future—what was to happen next—that mattered.

The *Pollux* had stood guard over the ruined fortress of Caliban until the relief ships arrived. Now she was homeward bound. At Lunar Base a richly deserved and long-postponed rest awaited her and her men. And there was not a man on board but would have a wife or sweetheart waiting for him at the receiving dock. Leave and liberty were ahead, and since it was impossible to spend money in the ship's canteen, every member of the crew had a year's or more accrued pay on the books. Moreover there would be bonuses and prize money for the destruction of the Ziffler gang. Never in the history of the service had a ship looked forward to such a satisfactory homecoming, for everyone at her arrival would be gaily waving bright handkerchiefs, laughing and smiling. Her chill mortuary chamber down below was empty, as were the neat rows of bunks in the sick bay. The *Pollux* had achieved her triumph without casualties.

It was on that happy day of making port that Bullard was idly dreaming when the sharp double rap on the door informed him that Moore was back. And the executive officer would hardly have come back so soon unless something important had turned up. So when Bullard jerked himself upright again and saw the pair of yellow flimsies in Moore's hand, his heart sank at once. Orders. Orders and always more orders! Would they never let the ship rest?

"Now what?" asked Bullard warily.

"The Bureau of Justice," said Moore, laying down the first signal, "has just ordered the immediate payment to all hands of the Ziffler bonus. It runs into handsome figures."

Bullard grunted, ignoring the message. Of course. The men would get a bonus and a handsome one. But why at this particular moment? He knew that Moore was holding back the bad news.

"Go on," growled Bullard, "let's have it!"

Moore shuffled his feet unhappily, expecting an outburst of rage. Then, without a word he handed Bullard the second message. It read:

> *Pollux* will stop at Juno Skydocks en route Luna to have hull scraped. Pay crew and grant fullest liberty while there. Implicit compliance with this order expected.
>
> GRAND ADMIRAL.

Bullard glared at the thing, then crushed it to a tight ball in his fist and hurled it from him. He sat for a moment cursing softly under his breath during which the red haze of rage almost blinded him. He would have preferred anything to that order—to turn about and go out of the orbit of Neptune for another battle, if there had been need for it, would have been preferable. But this!

He kicked his chair backward and began pacing the room like a caged tiger. It was such a lousy, stinking trick to do—and to him and his *Pollux* of all people! To begin with, the ship had no sky-barnacles on her hull, as the pestiferous little ferrous-consuming interplanetary spores were

called on account of the blisters they raised on the hull.
And if she had, Juno was no place to get rid of them. Its
skydock was a tenth-rate service station fit only for tugs and
mine layers. The twenty men employed there could not possibly be expected to go over the hull under a month, and
the regulations forbade the ship's crew working on the hull
while in a planetary dockyard. The dockyard workers'
guilds had seen to that. Moreover, Juno was not even on
the way to Luna, but far beyond, since from where the
Pollux was at the moment, the Earth lay between her and
the Sun, while Juno was in opposition. It was damnable!

Bullard growled in midstride and kicked viciously at an
electrician's testing case that stood in his path. That wasn't
all—not by a damsite! Juno was one of the vilest dumps
inside the Federation. It was an ore-gathering and provi-
sioning point for the asteroid prospectors and consequently
was populated by as vicious a mob of beachcombers and
their ilk as could be found in the System. Juno literally
festered with gin mills, gambling hells and dives of every
description. No decent man could stand it there for three
days. He either left or took to drink. And, what with what
was sold to drink on Juno, that led to all the rest—ending
usually in drugs or worse. It was in that hell hole that he
had been ordered to set down his fine ship for thirty days.
When he thought of his fine boys and the eager women impatiently awaiting their homecoming, he boiled.

"Shall I protest the order, sir?" asked Moore, hopefully.

"Certainly not," snapped Bullard, halting abruptly and
facing him. "I never protest orders. I carry 'em out. Even if

the skies fall. I'll carry this one out, too, damn 'em. But I'll make the fellow who dictated it—"

He suddenly checked himself. He had been about to add, "regret he ever had," when he remembered in a flash that Moore's family was in some way connected with the Fennings. Only Senator Fenning could have inspired the change of plans. The grand admiral had issued the order and signed it, of course, but he had inserted the clue as to why in its own last redundant sentence. "Implicit compliance is expected," indeed! No admiral would be guilty of such a tacit admission that perhaps not all orders need be strictly complied with. That sentence meant, as plainly as if the crude words themselves had been employed, this:

"Bullard, old boy, we know this looks goofy and all wrong to you, but we're stuck. You've been chosen as the sacrificial goat this year, so be a good sport and take it. None of your tricks, old fellow. We know you can dope out a way to annul any fool order, but don't let us down on this one."

The line of Bullard's mouth tightened. He sat down quietly in his chair and said to the expectant Moore as matter-of-factly as if he had been arranging a routine matter:

"Have the course changed for Juno, and inform the admiral that he can count on his orders being carried out to the letter."

Commander Moore may have been surprised at Bullard's tame surrender, but, after all, one was more helpless sometimes in dealing with one's own admiral than with the most ruthless and resourceful enemy. He merely said, "Aye, aye, sir," and left the room.

Two weeks rolled by, and then another. They were well within the orbit of Jupiter now, and indeed the hither asteroids. Hungry eyes now and then looked at the pale-blue tiny disk with its silvery dot companion as it showed on the low-power visifield and thought of home. Home was so near and yet so far. For the ship was veering off to the left, to pass close inside Mars and then to cut through beyond the Sun and far away again to where the miserable little rock of Juno rolled along with its nondescript population.

During those days the usual feverish activity of the ship died down until it became the dullest sort of routine. Men of all ratings were thinking, "What's the use?" Moore and Benton were everywhere, trying to explain away the unexplainable, but the men did not react very well. Many were beginning to wonder whether the service was what it was cracked up to be, and not a few were planning a big bust the very first night they hit the beach on Juno. It was not what they had planned, but it seemed to be what was available. Only Bullard and Lieutenant MacKay kept apart and appeared to take little interest in what was to happen next.

Alan MacKay was a newcomer to the service, and his specialty was languages. So he had filled in what time he had to spare from the routine duties by frequenting the prison spaces and chatting with the Callistans in the brig. He had managed to compile an extraordinary amount of

information relating to the recent war as seen from behind
the scenes on the other side, and he was sure it was going
to be of value to the Department. Moreover, he had gleaned
additional data on the foray to Oberon. All of which would
make the prosecutor's job more thorough when the day of
the trial came. As for Bullard, he kept to his cabin, pacing
the deck for hours at a stretch and wrestling with his newest
problem.

His thoughts were leaping endlessly in a circuit from
one item to the next and on and on until he came back to
the point of departure and began all over again. There was
the ship, the crew, and the devoted women waiting for the
return of the crew, and the fat entries in the paymaster's
books that meant so much to them both. And there was the
squalid town of Herapolis with its waiting, hungry harpies
with a thousand proven schemes for getting at that money
for themselves; and there was the cunning and avaricious
overlord of the asteroids, their landlord and creditor, who
would in the end transfer the funds to his own account.
That man also sat in the upper chamber of the Federation
Grand Council and was a power in Interplanetary politics.
His name was Fenning—*Senator* Fenning—and he dom-
inated the committee that dealt out appropriations to the
Patrol Force. And from that point Bullard's mind would
jump to the Tellurian calendar and he would recall that it
was now March on Earth, and therefore just about the time
that the annual budget was in preparation. Which in turn
would lead him back to the General Service Board, which
dealt on the one hand with the Force as a master, but with

the Grand Council as perennial supplicant for funds on
the other. Which naturally took him to the necessities of the
grand admiral and the needs of the Service as a whole.
Which brought him back to the *Pollux's* orders and started
the vicious circle all over again.

For Bullard was cynical and wise enough in the ways
of the world to have recognized at the outset that the ship's
proposed stay at Juno yard was neither more nor less than
a concealed bribe to the honorable senator. Perhaps it had
been a bad season in the asteroid mines and his debtors had
gotten behind. If so, they would need a needling of good,
honest cash to square accounts. Perhaps it was merely
Fenning's insatiable lust for ever more money, or maybe
he only insisted on the maneuver to demonstrate his authority. Or perhaps, even, having bulldozed the Patrol
Force into erecting a small and inadequate skydock where
either an effective one or none at all was needed, he felt
he must have some use made of it to justify his prior action.
Whatever Fenning's motives really were, they were ignoble.
No exigency of the service required the *Pollux* to visit
Juno now—or ever. And to Bullard's mind, no exigency of
politics or personal ambition could condone what was about
to be done to the *Pollux's* crew.

It was the ethical content of the problem that bothered
Bullard. Practically it was merely annoying. With himself on board, his veteran officers and a not inconsiderable
nucleus of tried and true men who had been in the ship for
years, she could not go altogether to hell no matter how
long they had to stay on Juno. He knew he could count on

many—perhaps half—going ashore only occasionally; the other half could be dealt with sternly should they exceed all reasonable bounds for shore behavior after a hard and grueling cruise. But in both halves he would have to deal with discontent. The decent, far-sighted, understanding men already resented the interference with their plans, since there was no sufficiently plausible reason given for it. They would accept it, as men have from the beginning of time, but not gracefully or without grumbling. Then the riotous element would feel, if unduly harsh disciplinary measures were applied, that, somehow, they had been let down. Wasn't the very fact that they had been sent to Juno for liberty and paid off with it an invitation to shoot the works?

There were other courses of action open to him, Captain Bullard knew. The easiest was inaction. Let the men have their fling. Given a few months in space again, he could undo all the damage. All? That was it. Nothing could undo the disappointment of the women waiting at Earth and Luna—nor the demoralization of the men at not getting there, for that matter. Nor could the money coaxed or stolen from them by the Junoesque creatures of Fenning ever be recovered. Moreover, the one thing Bullard did not like was inaction. If he was already half mutinous himself, what of the men? No. He would do something about it.

Well, he could simply proceed to Luna, take the blame, and perhaps be dismissed. He could give the story to the magnavox in the hope that by discrediting Senator Fenning and the System, his sacrifice might be worth the making. But would it? Would the magnavox dare put such a story on the ether? And wouldn't that be letting the admirals down? For they knew his dilemma quite as well as he did. They had chosen, chosen for the good of the Service. The System could *not* be broken, or it would have been long ago. It was the *Pollux's* turn to contribute the oil that greased the machine.

Bullard sighed. Juno was less than a week away now, and he saw no way out. Time after time in his gloom he was almost ready to admit he was beaten. But the instincts and training of a lifetime kept him from the actual confession. There must be some way of beating Fenning! It must be a way, of course, which would cast no reflection on the grand admiral. Or the ship. Or the crew. And, to be really successful, no ineradicable discredit upon himself. Bullard got up, rumpled his hair, and resumed his tigerish pacing.

It was Lieutenant MacKay who interrupted his stormy thoughts. MacKay had something to say about the prisoners. He had just about finished pumping them dry and was prepared to draw up the report. There were several recommendations he had to make, but he wanted his captain's opinion and approval first.

"It's about that fellow Zander—the Earthman, you know—" he began.

"Oh, Brimstone Bill?" grinned Bullard. He was rather glad MacKay had broken in on him. The sense of futility he had been suffering lately had begun to ingrow and make him bitter.

"Yes, sir. He's a highly undesirable citizen, of course, but I'm beginning to feel a little sorry for him. The old scalawag hadn't anything to do with the Caliban massacre. He just happened to be there when Ziffler came, and escaped being killed only by luck. He was dealer in a *rango* game when they landed, and his boss had a couple of Callistan bouncers. Ziffler gave 'em the chance of joining up with him, which they did and took Brimstone along with 'em, saying he was okay. Brimstone went along because it was that or else. He had no part in anything."

"I see," said Bullard, and thought a moment. "But I haven't anything to do with it. What happens hereafter is up to the court. You should submit your report to them."

After MacKay left, Bullard's thoughts turned upon his first encounter with the little charlatan many years before on Venus. Somehow, the fellow had had a profound effect on him at the time. So much so, in fact, that it came as something of a shock the day of his preliminary examination to find that the man had been a fake all along. Bullard had been tempted to think him a good man who had eventually gone wrong. Now he knew better. But as he continued his train of reminiscence, something suddenly clicked inside his head.

He sat bolt upright, and a gleam of hope began to dawn in his eyes. Brimstone Bill had a peculiar talent which might come in very handy in the trying weeks ahead. Could he use it with safety to himself? That had to be considered, for dealing with a professional crook had risks. Yet, according to Brimstone's own admission, it had been a gormel engineer that had shown him up, and Bullard figured that if a biophysics engineer could match wits with the grizzled trickster and win, he could. Perhaps—

But there was no perhaps about it. Bullard's fingers were already reaching for his call button, and a moment later Benton stood before him.

"Go down to the brig," directed the captain, "and bring that man Zander up here. Take his irons off first as I do not like to talk to men bound like animals. The fellow is a cheap crook, but he is harmless physically."

While he waited for Benton's return, Bullard explored the plan he had already roughly outlined in his mind. By pitting Brimstone Bill against Fenning he hoped to foil the greater scoundrel. But would he fall between two stools in the doing of it? He must also pit himself against the swindler, or else he would simply have enabled one crook to outsmart another without profit other than the gratification of spite. He had also to think of the other possible costs. The grand admiral must have no cause for complaint that there had been any evasion of his orders. Likewise Fenning must have no grievance that he dared utter out loud. There remained the item of the reputation of the *Pollux* and its men.

He puckered his brow for a time over that one. Then he relaxed. There were reputations and reputations, and extremes both ways. Some regarded one extreme with great favor, others preferred the other. Bullard liked neither, but for practical reasons preferred to embrace one for a time rather than its alternate. He would chance a little ridicule. After all, people might smile behind their hands at what a Polliwog might do, but no one ever curled a lip in the face of one and afterward had his face look the same. *Pollux* men had quite a margin of reputation, when it came to that, so he dismissed the matter from his mind. From then on he sat and grinned or frowned as this or that detail of his proposed course of action began to pop out in anticipation.

When Brimstone Bill was brought in, there was no hint in Bullard's bearing that he had softened his attitude toward the prisoner one whit. He stared at him with cold, unsmiling sternness.

"Zander," he said, drilling him with his eyes, "you are in a bad jam. Do you want to die along with those other gorillas?"

"Oh, no, sir," whined Brimstone, "I'll do anything. . . . I'll spill all I know. . . . I'd—"

Bullard shut him off with an abrupt wave of the hand.

"As the arresting officer I am in a position to do you a great deal of good or harm. If you will play ball with me, I can guarantee you a commutation. Maybe more—much more." He uttered the last words slowly as if in some doubt as to how much more. "Will you do it?"

"Oh, sir," cried Brimstone in an ecstasy of relief, for it was plain to see he had suffered during his languishment in the brig, "I'll do anything you say—"

"On *my* terms?" Bullard was hard as a rock.

"On any terms— Oh, yes, sir . . . just tell me—"

"Benton! Kindly leave us now while I talk with this man. Stay close to the call signal."

Bullard never took his eyes off the receding back of his lieutenant until the door clicked to behind it. Then he dropped his hard-boiled manner like a mask.

"Sit down, Brimstone Bill, and relax. I'm more friendly to you than you think." He waved to a chair and Brimstone sat down, looking a little frightened and uncertain. Then, proceeding on the assumption that a crook would understand an ulterior motive where he would distrust an honest one, Bullard dropped his voice to a low conversational—or rather conspiratorial—tone, and said:

"Everybody needs money. You do. And—well, a captain of a cruiser like this has obligations that the admiralty doesn't think about. *I* could use money, too. You are a clever moneymaker and can make it in ways I can't. I'm going to let you out of the jug and put you in the way of making some."

Brimstone Bill was keenly listening now and the glint of greed brightened his foxy eyes. This man in uniform was talking his language; he was a fellow like himself—no foolishness about him. Brimstone furtively licked his lips. He had had partners before, too, and that usually worked out pretty well, also. He might make a pretty good bargain yet.

"We are on our way to Juno where we will stop awhile. I am going to let you go ashore there and do your stuff.

You'll be given my protection, you can keep the money here in my safe, and you can sleep here nights. You had a pretty smooth racket there on Venus, as I remember it. If you work it here, we'll clean up. After we leave, we'll split the net take fifty-fifty. That'll give you money enough to beat the charges against you and leave you a stake. All I want you to do is preach the way you did on Venus."

While Bullard was talking, Brimstone grew brighter and brighter. It was beginning to look as if the world was his oyster. But at the last sentence he wilted.

"I can't do that," he wailed. "I'm afraid. And—"

"There are no gormel mills on Juno," Bullard reminded him, "only roughneck asteroid miners, gamblers and chiselers."

"That ain't it, sir," moaned Brimstone. "They smashed my gadgets, 'n'—"

"Gadgets?"

"Yeah. I ain't no good without 'em. And the fellow that made 'em is dead."

He talked on a few minutes more, but Bullard interrupted him. He called in Benton and told him to take notes.

"Go on," he told Brimstone Bill. "We'll make you a set."

It took about an hour before Benton had all the information he needed. Brimstone was hazy as to some of the features of his racket, but Bullard and the young officer were way ahead of him all the time.

"Can do?" asked Bullard, finally.

"Can do," declared Benton with a grin, slamming his notebook shut. "I'll put the the boys in the repair shop right at it. They won't have the faintest notion what we want to use 'em for."

Benton rose. As far as that went, Benton himself was still somewhat in the fog, but he had served with his skipper long enough to know that when he was wearing a certain, inward kind of quizzical expression something out of the ordinary was cooking. His talent for a peculiar oblique approach to any insoluble problem was well known to those about him. Wise ones did as they were told and asked questions, if ever, afterward.

"On your way out, Benton," added Bullard, "take our friend down to the chaplain's room—we left Luna in such a hurry, you know, the chaplain missed the ship—and let him bunk there. I'll see that suitable entry is made in the log. And you might tell Commander Moore that I'd like to see him."

When Benton and Brimstone had left, Bullard leaned back in his chair and with hands clasped behind his neck gazed contemplatively at the overhead. So far, so good. Now to break the news to Moore.

"I've been thinking, Moore," he said, when his executive came in, "that we have been a little lax in one matter. I was thinking of . . . uh, spiritual values. I'm sorry now that the chaplain missed the ship. Do you realize that we have made no pretense at holding any sort of service since we blasted off on this cruise?"

Moore's eyes bugged a little. The skipper, he was thinking, must have overdone his recent worrying. Or something. Bullard had always been punctiliously polite to the chaplain, but—

"So," went on Bullard calmly, still gazing placidly at the maze of wires and conduits hanging from the deck plates over him, "I have made appropriate arrangements to rectify that lack. I find that the Earthman we took along with the Ziffler outfit was not one of them but a hostage they had captured. He is an itinerant preacher—a freelance missionary, so to speak. I have released him from the brig and installed him in the chaplain's room, and after he has had a chance to clean up and recover, he will talk to the men daily."

It was well that Moore's eyes were firmly tied to their sockets, for if they had bugged before, they bulged dangerously now. Bullard had brooded too much. Bullard was mad!

"Oh," assured Bullard, "there is nothing to worry about. The man is still a prisoner at large awaiting action by the Bureau of Justice. But otherwise he will have the run of the ship. And, I should add, the run of the town while we are on Juno. He calls himself, oddly enough, Brimstone Bill, but he explains that he works close to the people and they prefer less dignity."

Moore gasped, but there seemed to be nothing to say. Bullard had not consulted him, he had been merely telling him. Unless he had the boldness to pronounce his captain unwell and forcibly assume command, there was nothing to do but accept it. And with a husky, "Aye, aye," he did.

It was the night before they made Juno that the long un-heard twitter of bos'n's pipes began peeping and cheeping throughout the ship. At the call, the bos'n's mates took up the cry and the word, "Rig church in the fo'c's'le ri-ight a-awa-a-ay!" went resounding through the compartments. Bullard clung tenaciously to the immemorial old ship customs. The sound of bunks being cleared away and the clatter of benches being put up followed as the crew's living quarters were transformed into a temporary assembly hall. They had been told that the missionary brought aboard at Oberon had a message for them. They had not been told what its subject was, but their boredom with black space was immense and they would have gone, anyway, if only from curiosity. The text for the evening was "The Gates of Hell Are Yawning Wide."

Two hours earlier Benton had reported that all was in readiness for the test of Brimstone's persuasive powers and that the three petty officer assistants picked by him had been instructed in their job. A special box had been rigged at one corner of the hall for the use of the captain and executive. Consequently, when "Assembly" went, Bullard waited only long enough for the men to be seated when he marched in with Moore and took his place at one corner of the stage that had been set up.

Brimstone Bill appeared in a solemn outfit made up for him by the ship's tailor. The setting and the clothes had made a new man of him. No longer was he the shifty-looking, cringing prisoner, but a man of austerity and power whose flashing eyes more than made amends for his poor physique. He proceeded to the center of the stage, glared at his audience a moment, then flung an accusing finger at them.

"Hell is waiting for you!" he exploded, then stepped back and shook his imposing mane and continued to glare at them. There was not a titter or sneer in the crowd. The men were sitting upright, fascinated, looking back at him with staring eyes and mouths agape. He had hit them where they lived. Moore looked about him in a startled way and nudged Bullard.

"Can you tie that?" he whispered, awestruck. He had been in the ship many years and had never seen anything like it. All the skymen he knew had been more concerned with the present and the immediate future than the here-after, and the Polliwogs were no exception.

Brimstone Bill went on. Little by little he warmed to his subject until he soon arrived at a stage where he ranted and raved, jumped up and down, tore his hair and beat his breast. He thundered denunciations, pleaded and threat-ened, storming all over the place purple-faced. His auditors quailed in their seats as he told off their shortcomings and predicted the dire doom that they were sure to achieve. His list of punishable iniquities was simple. The cardinal sins were the ordinary personal petty vices—drinking, smoking, gambling, dancing and the like. There was but one redeem-ing virtue: *Support the cause!*

That was all there was to it. An hour of exhortation and a collection. When he paused at the end of his culminating outpouring of fiery oratory, he asked for volunteers to gather in the offerings. Three petty officers stood up, received commodious leather bags, and went among the audience stuffing them with whatever the men present had in their pockets. For no one withheld anything, however trifling. The sermon, if it could be called that, was an impressive success. Then the lights came on bright, Brimstone Bill left the stage clutching the three bags, and the men filed out.

"Amazing," said Moore, as he sat with Bullard and watched the show. "Why, the fellow is an arrant mountebank!"

"Quite so," agreed Bullard, "but the men seem to like it. Come, let's go."

The next day saw a very different atmosphere in the ship. About two thirds of the crew had heard the preaching, the remainder being on duty. Those went about their tasks silently and thoughtfully, as if pondering their manifold sins. They had to take an enormous amount of kidding from their shipmates and a good many black eyes were in evidence by the time the ship slid down into her landing skids at Juno Skydock. Bullard did not let that disturb him; to him it was a healthful sign.

As soon as the ship was docked, he went out and met the dockmaster, who, as he had suspected, was an incompetent drone. No, he had only fourteen men available—he had not been expecting the ship—they would get at the job tomorrow or next day—or at least part of them. No, there was a local rule against working overtime—no, the ship's force could not help—six Earth weeks, he thought, barring accidents, ought to do the trick. Oh, yes, they would be very thorough. At Juno they were always thorough about everything.

Moore started threatening the man, stating he would report him to the grand admiral for inefficiency, but all Bullard said was:

"Skip it, you're wasting breath. These people have just two speeds—slow ahead and stop. Put pressure on them and they backfire. Go back aboard and post the liberty notice. Unlimited liberty except for the men actually needed to stand watch. And see that this goat gets a copy."

Moore shook his head. Something *had* happened to Bullard. Of course, the man was up against a stone wall, but he could at least make a show of a fight. It was a terrible thing to see a fighting man give up so easily. In the meantime Bullard had walked away and was talking with Brimstone Bill and Benton, who had just emerged from the lock and were looking around.

There were lively doings ashore that night. Most of the contingent that had not heard the Reverend Zander's moving sermon went as early as possible, ostensibly to look around and do a little shopping. In the end they wound up by getting gloriously drunk. It was a bedraggled and miserable-looking lot that turned up at the ship the next morning and there were many stragglers. A patrol had to be sent out to comb the dives and find the missing ones. Many had been robbed or cheated of all they had, and some had been indiscreet enough to draw all their money before they went. Captain Bullard lined up the most serious of the offenders at "mast" and handed out the usual routine punishments—a few days' restriction to the ship.

After that things were different. The next day Benton and Brimstone had succeeded in renting an empty dance hall. As Bullard had guessed, things were dull that year in Herapolis. A gang of enthusiastic volunteers—Polliwog converts to Brimstone's strange doctrines—busied themselves in making the place ready as a tabernacle. The last touch was a neon sign bearing the same wording Bullard had seen on that other tabernacle in steamy Venus. Brimstone Bill was about to do his stuff in a wholesale way.

That afternoon when work was done, the entire liberty party marched in formation to the hall and there listened to another of Brimstone's fiery bursts of denunciation. The denizens of the town looked on at the swinging legs and arms of the marching battalion and wondered what it was all about. They supposed it was some newfangled custom of the Patrol Force and that whatever it was, it would soon be over and then they would have plenty of customers. The barkeeps got out their rags and polished the bars and gamblers made a last-minute check-up of the magnetic devices that controlled their machines.

But no customers came that night. For hours they could hear the booming, ranting voice of Brimstone roaring about Hell and Damnation, punctuated by periods of lusty singing, but except for an occasional bleary-eyed miner, no patron appeared to burden their tills and lighten their hearts. At length the strange meeting broke up and the men marched back to their ship in the same orderly formation they had come.

This went on for a week. A few at a time, the members of the first liberty party recovered from their earlier debauch and ventured ashore again, but even those were soon snatched from circulation as their shipmates persuaded them to hear Brimstone "just once." Once was enough. After that they joined the nocturnal demonstration. It was uncanny. It was unskymanlike. Moreover, it was lousy business. Spies from the townspeople's camp who peered through windows came back and reported there was something funnier about it than that. Every night a collection was taken up, and it amounted to big money, often requiring several men to carry the swag back.

Strong-arm squads searched the town's flophouses to find out where the pseudo-evangelist was staying, but in vain. They finally discovered he was living on the *Pollux*. A committee of local "merchants" called on Captain Bullard and protested that the ship was discriminating against them by curtailing the men's liberty. They also demanded that Brimstone Bill be ejected from the ship.

"Practically the entire crew goes ashore every day," said Bullard shortly, "and may spend the night if they choose. What they do ashore is their own affair, not mine. If they prefer to listen to sermons instead of roistering, that's up to them. As far as the preacher is concerned, he is a refugee civilian, whose safety I am responsible for. He is in no sense under orders of the Patrol Force. If you consider you have a competitive problem, solve it in your own way."

The dive owners' impatience and perplexity turned into despair. Something had to be done. They did all that they knew to do. They next complained to the local administrator—a creature of Fenning's—of the unfair competition. That worthy descended upon the tabernacle shortly thereafter, backed by a small army of suddenly acquired deputies, to close the place as being an unlicensed entertainment. He was met by a determined Patrol lieutenant and a group of hard-faced Polliwog guards who not only refused to permit the administrator to serve his warrant, but informed him that the meeting was immune from political interference. It was not amusement, but religious instruction, and as such protected by the Constitution of the Federation.

The astounded administrator looked at the steely eyes of the officer and down to the browned, firm hand lying carelessly on the butt of a Mark XII blaster, and back again into the granite face. He mumbled something about being sorry and backed away. He could see little to be gained by frontal attack. He went back to his office and sent off a hasty ethergram to his esteemed patron, then sat haggardly awaiting orders. Already the senator had made several inquiries as to receipts since the cruiser's arrival, but he had delayed reporting.

The answer was short and to the point. "Take direct

action," it said. The administrator scratched his head. Sure, he was the law on Juno, but the *Pollux* represented the law, too, and it had both the letter of it and the better force on its side. So he did the other thing—the obvious thing for a Junovian to do. He sent out a batch of ether-grams to nearby asteroids and then called a mass meeting of all his local henchmen.

It took three days for the armada of rusty little pros-pectors' ships to finish fluttering down onto the rocky wastes on the far side of Herapolis. They disgorged an army of tough miners and bruisers from every little rock in the vicinity. The mob that formed that night was both numerous and well-primed. Plenty of free drinks and the mutual display of flexed biceps had put them in the mood. At half an hour before the tabernacle meeting was due to break up, the dive keepers all shut up shop, and taking their minions with them began to line the dark streets be-tween Brimstone's hall and the skydock.

"Yah! Sissies!" jeered the mob, as the phalanx of blue-jackets came sweeping down, arm in arm and singing one of Brimstone's militant hymns in unison. By the dim street lights one could see that their faces were lit up with the self-satisfaction of the recently purified. In the midst of the phalanx the little preacher trotted along, surrounded by the inevitable trio of petty officers with the night's col-lection.

An empty bottle was flung, more jeers, and a volley of small meteoric stones. The column marched on, scorning to indulge in street brawling. Then a square ahead they came to the miners, drawn up in solid formation from wall to wall. The prospectors were armed with pick handles and other improvised clubs. They did not jeer, but stood silent and threatening.

"Wedge formation," called Benton, who was up ahead. "Charge!"

The battle of the Saints and Sinners will be remembered long in Juno. That no one was killed was due to the restraint exercised by Benton and MacKay, who were along with the church party. Only they and the administrator had blasters, and the administrator was not there. Having marshaled his army, he thought it the better part of valor to withdraw to his office where he could get in quick touch with the senator if need be.

Dawn found a deserted street, but a littered one. Splintered clubs, tattered clothes, and patches of drying blood abounded, but there were no corpses. The Polliwogs had fought their way through, carrying their wounded with them. The miners and the hoodlums had fled, leaving their wounded sprawling on the ground behind, as is the custom in the rough rocklets. But the wounded suffered only from minor broken bones or stuns, and sooner or later crawled away to some dive where they found sanctuary. There had been no referees, so there was no official way to counteract the bombastic claims at once set up by both sides. But it is noteworthy that the Polliwogs went to church again the next night and were unmolested by so much as a catcall on the way back.

"I don't like this, captain," Moore had said that morning as they looked in on the crowded sick bay where the doctors were applying splints and bandages. "I never have felt that charlatan could be anything but bad for the ship. He gouges the men just as thoroughly as the experts here would have. Now this!"

"They would have thrown their money around, anyway," grinned Bullard, "and fought, too. It's better to do both sober than the other way."

That afternoon the administrator rallied his bruised and battered forces and held a council of war. None would admit it, but a formation has advantages over a heterogeneous mob even in a free-for-all. What to do next? There was a good deal of heated discussion, but the ultimate answer was—infiltration. The tabernacle sign read, "Come one, come all," and there was no admission. So that night the hall was surrounded by waiting miners and a mob of the local bouncers long before Zander arrived. Tonight they would rough-house inside.

He beamed upon them.

"Come in, all of you. There are seats for all. If not, my regular boys can stand in the back."

The roughs would have preferred the standing position, but the thing was to get in and mix. So they filed in. By the time Brimstone Bill mounted the rostrum the house was crowded, but it could have held more at a pinch.

He was in good form that night. At his best. "Why Risk Damnation?" was his theme, and as he put it, the question was unanswerable. It was suicidal folly. The gaping miners let the words soak in with astonished awe; never had they thought of things that way. Here and there a bouncer shivered when he thought of the perpetual fires that were kept blazing for him on some faraway planet called Hell. They supposed it must be a planet—faroff places usually were. They were not a flush lot, but their contribution to the "cause" that night was not negligible. There was little cash money in it, but a number of fine nuggets, and more than one set of brass knuckles and a pair of nicely balanced blackjacks. Altogether Brimstone Bill was satisfied with his haul, especially when he saw the rapt expressions on their faces as they made their way out of the tabernacle.

The administrator raved and swore, but it did no good. The chastened miners were down early at the smelter office to draw what credits they had due; the bouncers went back to their dives and quit their jobs, insisting on being paid off in cash, not promises. All that was for the cause. There were many fights that day between groups of the converted and groups of the ones who still dwelt in darkness, but the general results were inconclusive. The upshot of it was that the remainder of the town went to the tabernacle that night to find out what monkey business had been pulled on the crowd they had sent first.

The collection that night was truly stupendous, for the sermon's effect on the greater crowd was just what it had been on all the others. Not only was there a great deal of cash, but more weapons and much jewelry—though a good deal of the jewelry upon examination turned out to be

paste. The administrator had come—baffled and angry—
to see for himself. He saw, and everyone was surprised to
note how much cash he carried about his person. What no
one saw was the ethergram he sent off to the senator that
night bearing his resignation and extolling the works of one
Brimstone Bill, preacher extraordinary. He was thankful
that he had been shown the light before it was too late.

An extraordinary by-product of the evening was that
early the next morning a veritable army of miners descended upon the skydock and volunteered to help scrape
the cruiser's hull. Brimstone's dwelling, they said, should
shine and without delay. That night even the dockmaster
had to grudgingly pronounce that the ship was clean. The
job was done. She was free to go.

Bullard lost no time in blasting out. Brimstone Bill was
tearful over leaving the last crop ungleaned. He insisted
that they had been caught unawares the first night, and
the second they were sure to bring more. But Bullard said
no, they had enough money for both their needs. The ship
could stay no longer. Bullard further said that he would
be busy with the details of the voyage for the next several
days. After that they would have an accounting. In the
meantime there would be no more preaching. Brimstone
Bill was to keep close to his room.

At once all the fox in Brimstone rose to the top. This
man in gold braid had used him to exploit not only his
own crew but the people of an entire planetoid and adjacent
ones. Now he was trying to cheat him out of his share of
the take.

"I won't do it," said Brimstone, defiantly. "I've the run of the ship, you said. If you try to doublecross me, I'll spill everything."

"Spill," said Bullard calmly, "but don't forget what happened at Venus. The effect of the gadgets wears off, you know. I *think* you will be safe in the chaplain's room if I keep a guard on the door. But if you'd rather, there's always the brig—"

"I get you," said Brimstone Bill, sullenly, and turned to go. He knew now he had been outsmarted, which was a thing that hurt a man who lived by his wits.

"You will still get," Bullard hurled after him, "one half the net, as I promised you, and an easy sentence or no sentence at all. Now get out of my sight and stay out."

It was a queer assembly that night—or sleep period— for a space cruiser of the line. They met in the room known to them as the "treasure house." Present were the captain, the paymaster, Lieutenant Benton, and two of the petty officers who had acted as deacons of Brimstone's strange church. The third was missing for the reason he was standing sentry duty before the ex-preacher's door. Their first job was to count the loot. The money had already been sorted and piled, the paper ten to one hundred sol notes being bundled neatly, and the small coins counted into bags. The merchandise had been appraised at auction value and was stacked according to kind.

"Now let's see, Pay," said Bullard, consulting his notes,

"what is the total amount the men had on the books before we hit Juno?"

Pay told him. Bullard kicked at the biggest stack of money of all.

"Right. This is it. Put it in your safe and restore the credits. Now, how much did the hall cost, sign, lights and all?"

Bullard handed that over.

"The rest is net—what we took from the asteroid people. Half is mine, half is Brimstone's. The total?"

Benton was looking uneasy. He had wondered all the time about what the fifty-fifty split meant. He was still wondering what the skipper meant to do with his. But the skipper was a queer one and unpredictable.

"Fifty-four thousand, three hundred and eight sols," said the paymaster, "including the merchandise items."

"Fair enough. Take that over, too, into the special account. Then draw a check for half of it to Brimstone. Put the other half in the ship's amusement fund. They've earned it. They can throw a dance with it when we get to Luna. I guess that's all."

Bullard beckoned Benton to follow and left the storeroom, leaving the two p. o.'s to help the paymaster cart the valuables away to his own bailiwick. There were still other matters to dispose of. Up in the cabin Benton laid the "gadgets" on the desk.

"What will I do with these, sir?" he wanted to know. "They're honeys! I hate to throw them into the disintegrator."

"That is what you will do, though," said Bullard. "They are too dangerous to have around. They might fall into improper hands."

"Now that it's over, would you mind telling me how these worked?"

"Not at all. We've known for a century that high-frequency sound waves do queer things, like reducing glass to powder. They also have peculiar effects on organisms. One frequency kills bacteria instantly, another causes red corpuscles to disintegrate. You can give a man fatal anemia by playing a tune to him he cannot hear. These gadgets are nothing more than supersonic vibrators of different pitch such that sounded together they give an inaudible minor chord that affects a portion of the human brain. When they are vibrated along with audible speech, the listener is compelled to believe implicitly in every word he hears. The effect persists for two or three days. That is why I say they are too dangerous to keep. Brimstone could just as well have incited to riot and murder as preach his brand of salvation for the money it brought."

"I see. And the ones carried in our pockets by me and the boys were counter-vibrators, so we didn't feel the effects?"

"Yes. Like the ones you rigged in my box that night we had the tryout up forward. Neither I nor Commander Moore heard anything but ranting and drivel."

"Pretty slick," said Benton.

Yes, pretty slick, thought Bullard. He had stayed the prescribed time on Juno and had paid off the crew and granted full liberty. Outside the five men in his confidence, not a member of the crew had had a hint that it was not desired that he go ashore and waste his money and ruin his health.

"I'm thinking that the *Pollux* is not likely to be ordered back to Juno soon," said Bullard absently. But Benton wasn't listening. He was scratching his head.

"That little guy Brimstone," he said. "He isn't such a bad egg, come to think of it. Now that he's pulled us out of our hole, do you think you can get him out of this, sir?"

"He never was in the hole," said Bullard, reaching for the logbook. "I needn't have kept him at all once I let him out of the brig. Read it—it was on your watch and you signed it."

Benton took the book and read.

> At 2204 captain held examination of prisoners; remanded all to brig to await action of the Bureau of Justice except one Ignatz Zander, Earthman. Zander was released from custody, but will be retained under Patrol jurisdiction until arrival at base in the event the Bureau should wish to utilize him as witness.

Benton looked puzzled.

"I don't remember writing anything like that," he said.

"The official final log is prepared in this office," reminded Bullard softly. "You evidently don't read all you sign."

*When the war is over peace is signed, and seldom
by the men most concerned. Then is a space navy blithely
shelved amid rosy promises—to be conveniently
forgotten by the diplomats. But when trouble threatens
then the buck is passed once more to the man of action.
So did Acting-Admiral Bullard find himself at this
stage in his career forced to issue the strangest of orders.*

ORDERS

· Being the world's worst thumb twiddler, Bullard was unhappy. He was restless, disgusted and bored. There was
nothing to do. There could be nothing to do. And if there
should be, by any chance, there was nothing to do it with.
That he temporarily bore the rank of admiral while acting
as commandant of the great Lunar Base helped him not
at all. He had little taste for brass-hattism and an immense
loathing for swivel chairs. He got up from the one he was
sitting in and paced the floor of his sumptuous office for
awhile. Then he planted himself before its big window and
stared gloomily at the dreary scene outside.

The uncanny silence in that former bustling place was
depressing. No longer was heard the shrill whistles of
traveling cranes, the whir of fabricating machines, or the

185

boom-boom of heavy stamps. The shops were closed; the men laid off; the ships away. Ships! Bullard's mouth tightened. Yes, there were ships present, rows upon rows of them—dead hulls of what had once been proud warships, now rusting away until the wrecking crews should come and go to work on them. What remnants of the Fleet had escaped the ax wielded by the gang of pacifists now in control were dispersed to the far corners of the System, their crews enjoying themselves on leisurely, junketing, "good-will cruises." His own good ship, the *Pollux*, was the sole exception. She lay at the moment over in the remodeling dock in Gobi Crater, her machinery torn out and the bulk of her crew disbanded. The amazing new astral drive units that were meant to go in her still lay unboxed in the storehouse, the nullochrons were not even on order. It might be a year before work was resumed. Bullard sighed. So this was the peace he had fought hard for. Bah!

Peace reigned from the flaming face of Sol to the outermost reaches of the Plutonian orbit. All was serene. Some claimed it would always be serene hereafter; the human race was fed up with war. There was never to be another one. Yes, peace. It was supposed to be wonderful, but Bullard felt otherwise. It was not that he was a war-loving man; far from it. But he knew his Martians, and his Callistans, and his Venusians, and all the rest, not forgetting some scheming Tellurians who dwelt down below on Earth. It was too much to expect that they would stay bound forever by the lofty phrases and noble sentiments expressed in the Treaty of Juno. It is true that they had forsworn the use of force in interplanetary relations, but the paths of history are littered with the torn scraps of similar treaties, though men seemed to have forgotten it. At any rate, the peace had borne heavily on the armed services. Officers and men were retired in droves, battleships and cruisers were enthusiastically scrapped, new construction came to a dead halt. There was nothing to look forward to but dull routine and inaction. Bullard sighed again, and gnawed his lower lip.

He was about to turn away from the window, weary from the bleak view and his own depressing thoughts, when his eye caught the glint of sunlight on burnished gold. The glitter came from a small sky-cycle that had just entered the dome through the southwest portal and was skimming to a stop in the middle of the parade ground. Bullard knew at once from its dark-green color that it belonged to the State Department, and from the golden insignia it sported that it was the personal car of a very high official. He frowned speculatively at that, for experience had taught him that unscheduled visits from diplomatic bigwigs invariably meant trouble. Their contempt for the Service was notorious—they haughtily ignored the uniformed men until their own muddlings sometimes brought affairs to such a pass that there was nothing left but to call in men of action to strengthen their hand.

"Wonder what this bird wants?" growled Bullard, watching the man alight from the machine. "If it's a snappy warship for a dirty job, he won't get it. There aren't any."

Then he put on his best poker face, recrossed the room, and sat down to await his caller.

"I," announced the caller, exuding pomposity and incompetence from every pore, "am Lionel Wallowby, Undersecretary of State for Asteroidal Affairs. My calling on you, rather than sending for you, though unprecedented—"

"I am honored," said Bullard, bowing stiffly, but without a quiver of expression. Now he knew whom he had to deal with, for Wallowby's name was a byword, and he knew that the interview was not going to be an easy one. Fellow officers who had dealt with the man complained afterward that the strain of holding themselves in was almost intolerable. Not that Wallowby was a villain, or even malicious. He was simply smug, vain, useless—an outstanding example of what nepotism at its worst can foist upon a suffering public.

"I come about a matter of great urgency which will require your immediate intervention."

"How can anything be urgent in these placid times?" asked Bullard bitterly, "and if so what can I do about it? Article VIII of the Treaty of Juno—of which, if my memory is not at fault, you were one of the drafters—forbids forever the use of force or the threat of force in any situation whatever; regardless of provocation. Isn't that correct?"

"Uh, yes," admitted Mr. Wallowby, squirming in his seat, "but there are aspects of the situation in hand that make it exceptional. You see, it is the attitude of the

Trojans. It is distressing. Humiliating. They sidestep, fence, and quibble. We have reached an impasse. An exasperating people, really."

"Quite!" said Bullard. He could think of a hundred adjectives applicable to them, all harsher. Exasperating, indeed! On the gray rocks of those far-off groups of asteroids lived the lowest and meanest dregs of mankind. Their rulers were fugitive shyster lawyers, disbarred from more decent planets. Their "aristocracy" were retired pirates and gamblers, their "working" populace a medley of every type of petty crook from pickpocket to cutthroat. Their very existence as a quasi-independent nation was a reproach to civilization.

"They take every advantage of their privileged international status," complained Mr. Wallowby.

"They would," said Bullard, dryly. "And why not?"

It was a dig at his caller, for it was Undersecretary Wallowby who had held out at the peace conference for the continued autonomy of the Trojans, alleging that to leave them as they were was the simplest evasion of the age-old rivalry between the Martians and the colonists on the Saturnian satellites. And so it might have been had the Trojans been populated by any other kind of people. But as it turned out, "autonomy," as construed by the bosses of the Trojans, meant license to thumb their noses at the rest of the civilized world. They owed their immunity to subjugation to their peculiar location in the Solar System. Both groups rode the orbit of Jupiter, one a half billion miles ahead, the other an equal distance behind the master planet. Therefore, the Jovians periodically made claim for jurisdiction. But there are years when Saturn is actually closer to one or the other of them, and often Mars is closer to both. From the earliest asteroid-grabbing days Mars and Saturn had quarreled over which had the primary interest. The nearsighted framers of the Treaty of Juno had ducked the issue by leaving the Trojan groups autonomous, but yet under the joint protection of both squabbling claimants. Whereupon the Trojans promptly made the most of it.

Bullard knew the rocky planetoids well, for he had visited them often in the days when manhunters were not handicapped by paralyzing rules. He knew the men who ran them, particularly the swashbuckling fourflusher who styled himself the Boss of Nestor. Since he had defied him more than once in cutting out some wanted man. But those good old days were gone. Nowadays the Trojans wrapped themselves in the blessing of the no-violence terms of the fatuous treaty. No one could enter their ports forcibly, or remove any criminal fugitive without their consent—not even one of their own protectors. Should Mars make harsh claims, the Trojans would appeal to the Saturnians, who in turn, could be counted upon to declare the Martians in the wrong. Or they would work it the other way around. On the other hand if the Earth or any other outside planet presented a claim or grievance, both protectors would be called in. The Trojans played both ends against the middle with great skill. Their position resembled that of certain small Balkan countries at an earlier period in history— they were of little intrinsic worth but of high nuisance value. The least upsetting of the status quo could easily initiate another general war. The Trojan situation, in short, was dynamite.

"What is your difficulty with the Trojans?" Bullard asked, seeing that Wallowby seemed at a loss to proceed. "What do you want of me?"

"I . . . uh, that is we . . . or the Department, I meant to say," stammered Wallowby, "find we are compelled to ask you to extricate . . . no, that isn't what I mean . . . *execute* a delicate diplomatic mission. It has to do with a notorious criminal known as Grory the Groat. We have extradited him and now want to secure custody."

"I have no ships in commission here," remarked Bullard, "whereas skyliners make the trip every month. Furthermore, you have a large staff of marshals who are maintained for just such missions. The apprehension of a civil prisoner is outside my jurisdiction." He had not missed Wallowby's fumbling of the word "extricate," and already guessed the civil arm had made a try for Grory and messed it up. Wallowby's capacity for bungling was unsurpassed.

"The Trojans do not treat our marshals with respect," whined Wallowby. He was not used to being talked back to, and he did not like to admit what he had to. "We have sent several, but they are always turned back on one legalistic pretext or another. In our first requisition we claimed Grory on charges of treason, sabotage, fomenting rebellion, and gun-running. They accepted it, but when our officer got there they told him that they had reconsidered. It appears that the crimes enumerated were not sufficient in view of the blanket amnesty clause in the Treaty."

"Of course not," said Bullard bluntly. "They have a political tinge. You should have known better. Isn't that general amnesty clause known widely as the Wallowby Provision?"

Wallowby flushed, then turned huffy.

"It was never intended to give immunity to common scoundrels of the Grory stripe," he said stiffly. "Moreover the treaty is not what I came to discuss."

Bullard shrugged. Wallowby went on.

"Since then we have submitted other requests. Five, to be exact. We have presented evidence of piracy, murder, and embezzlement. We have demanded him for smuggling drugs and white slaves, for counterfeiting, and a score of other crimes. Each time they say we may have him if we only send. Each time our marshal arrives there they send him back emptyhanded, always with a different excuse. To make the story short, they are evasive and uncooperative. They have persistently refused to arbitrate. They flout us, admiral, they flout us!" It was a wail.

"Maybe they don't *want* to give up Mr. Grory the Groat," said Bullard.

Wallowby looked momentarily startled as if that suggestion was entirely novel to him. Then he rallied himself and completed his oration.

"We have been correct, considerate, and courteous throughout. They repay us with legal sophistries. We have

dilly-dallied overlong. My patience is at its end. The hour
for action has struck. Now the time has come when we
must reveal the iron hand that lies beneath the velvet
glove—"

"*What* iron hand?" asked Bullard brutally.

Wallowby blinked and swallowed hard.

"Why, uh, the *potential* iron hand, of course. We must
be more impressive. We must be more stern. We must cease
making requests and make *demands*. You will at once send
a warship to Nestor and secure the person of this Grory
for us."

"That," said Bullard, rising, "is absolutely absurd. The
only ships we have that can take the void have been thoroughly demilitarized. Even if they were armed, we are still
forbidden by the terms of your ridiculous treaty from using
them. What, I ask, can a gunless battleship do that a letter
can't do?"

"You are impertinent, *Acting* Admiral Bullard," said
Wallowby with what was meant to be cutting sarcasm. He,
too, was on his feet, his face aflame. "I have wasted words
enough on you. Here are your orders. Carry them out."

He jerked a long official envelope from an inner pocket
and hurled it onto Bullard's desk. Then, after venting one
contemptuous sniff, stalked haughtily out.

"Well, I'll be—" whistled Bullard as the door closed
on the back of his departing caller.

He sat for long, staring down at those silly orders and
marveling at the incredible stupidity of a man such as

Wallowby. Yet, he asked himself after a time, was he so stupid after all? However he might bungle jobs, he had cunning enough to find an out. The suspicion was growing in Bullard's mind that this time it was he who had been chosen for the goat. He glanced through the orders again.

They were official enough, having been signed in open council by no lesser personage than the Director himself. And they were simple. They directed that a demilitarized man-of-war be put in commission at once and sent under the command of a competent officer to the port of Nestor in the Anterior Trojans. Upon arrival the ship's captain was to make peremptory demand upon the Boss of Nestor for the person of one Grory the Groat, receive him into custody, and deliver him to the appropriate authorities on Earth. The demand was to be made in the name of interplanetary law only and was not to be accompanied by threatening words or gestures. If refused, no efforts were to be made to apprehend Grory by force. In the latter event, the visiting officer was to politely withdraw and return to Luna.

"Nuts!" snorted Bullard, kicking his swivel chair out from under him and beginning a feverish pacing of the room. For five minutes he angrily strode up and down, cursing Wallowby without cessation. For now his dilemma was crystal clear. Wallowby, the louse, didn't matter any longer. He had adroitly ducked from under. The thing was official now. Whatever the stupidities and ineptness of the Office of Asteroidal Affairs, they had been buried, whitewashed, glossed-over, or what have you. The mess had been laid in Bullard's lap. It was his baby now. Worse, it was the Service's baby.

If and when the affair was ever made public, the story would run thus: Justice located their man; State put through the necessary requests and papers; Space Service was assigned to execute the ultimate act of physical possession. Whether or not they got the man would be irrelevant. The two civil departments had done their stuff, if blame was due it was due somewhere else.

"Heads he wins, tails I lose," growled Bullard. "If we get Grory, it is no more than we are expected to do—a routine matter; if we don't get Grory, we're a pack of bums. There isn't but one answer. No stuffed shirt like Wallowby is going to make this outfit a laughingstock as long as I'm giving the orders. *I'm going to get Grory.*"

He sat down to gather himself together and think of ways and means. The more he contemplated the problem, the thicker it got. Wallowby's legal sharks had done their best —and failed; his diplomats had made representations, argued and pleaded—and had failed; his marshals had been received with ridicule, and sent back defeated. But that, after all, was the Wallowby crowd. Bullard's eyes grew hard. He knew offhand of at least forty officers on the Moon he could send who would bring back Grory dead or alive, and the blustering Boss of Nestor, too, if it came to that, if only told to do so. But Bullard could not order them out. His hands were bound by the let-the-lamb-lie-down-with-the-lion platitudes of the accursed Treaty of Juno. No longer could a Guardsman look a hardboiled criminal in the eye and say, "Put 'em up, or else." Oh, no. You should approach the rogue politely and request he accompany you to the jail. Bah! That time Bullard picked up his chair and hurled it clear across the room. After that he took up his tigerish rug tramping again.

All the answers were negative. If he didn't bring Grory back, he would have furnished Wallowby with the alibi he sought. If he brought him back through the use of, or by the barest hint of force, a delicate interplanetary situation would be provoked. The Martians and Saturnians would be certain to protest it as a violation of the treaty, and again the blame would fall upon Bullard's man for having been overzealous. It might not result in a resumption of the war, but it was as risky as smoking in a powder magazine.

Spent from his excited pacing, Bullard sat down again. This time he discarded all the usual approaches and went at the problem in his own way. There had been other times in his life that he had received asinine, if not impossible, orders, and had managed somehow to carry them into execution, though, it must be admitted in all frankness, not always to the perfect satisfaction of those who had issued them. Now he must rack his brains again.

He scanned the list of ships present and the roster of personnel. The choice of ships was easy. He selected the ex-cruiser *Llerdyx*, a prize of war, for the vessel. Her guns had been pulled and the ports blanked off, and her torpedo tubes plugged beyond repair, but she was handy and fast and that was all he wanted. Bullard sent orderlies scurrying with word to various departments. The *Llerdyx* was to be renamed the *Texas Ranger*, provisioned and fueled and made ready for departure the following day. Her crew was to be made up of *Pollux* men then waiting in the lonely barracks by the Gobi dock.

All of Bullard's best officers were away on extended leave, but at length he found a notation on the roster that gave him comfort. Lieutenant Benton, whom he had fleeted up from tubeman, was due back on Luna that very night. Benton then was the man, for Benton could be relied upon. That disposed of the expedition except provision for what it was to do. That was the hardest task.

He sat down at the ordergraph. His fingers flew as he pecked out part one of the orders. They were largely a paraphrase of the set Wallowby brought. Then the going got hard; Bullard bogged down. He swore softly to himself, scowled, wrote pages and pages of drafts, only to tear them up and feed them into the maw of his wastebasket. He would light one cigarette on the butt of its predecessor, then grind it angrily under his heel. It was one thing to write orders that could be complied with, another to compose a set in the face of almost certain failure. It was like ordering a faithful follower to go up against a ruthless killer with nothing but an empty gun.

Dark was almost at hand when Bullard finally wrote out the words he dreaded to put down. But he did write them out, for his duty was plain. They would be painful for Benton to execute, and disgraceful for Bullard if they were ever made known. But the feelings and reputations of two men did not count in the grander scheme of things. Very reluctantly Bullard inserted the paper in an envelope, sealed it with a sigh, then typed on the cover these words:

> To be opened and put into effect only in the event that the Boss of Nestor refuses to hand over the person of Grory the Groat. Otherwise this must be returned to signer intact.
>
> Bullard.

An hour later Benton reported for duty, brisk, cheerful, and ruddy after his vacation. But his grin faded when he saw the somber mood of his skipper. Bullard hardly spoke. Instead he handed over part one of the orders.

"Gee!" said Benton, delighted. "I get a command. And do a cruise all on my own. That's great!"

"Evidently you do not understand what you are to do," said Bullard gravely.

"Sure. It's clear enough. I hop off tomorrow, go out to Nestor, tell 'em I want this bird Grory, slap him in the brig, and then come back. What's the catch?"

"They aren't going to give Grory up."

"Huh?" Benton was astonished. Then his face widened as his old grin came back. Now he knew—Bullard was having a little private fun, he was pulling his leg. "Why that flea-bitten little so-called republic. For two cents I'd blast 'em out of the ether, no matter what they've got."

"That," said Bullard, "is the hard part. You aren't permitted to do any blasting. You haven't any arms but sidearms. And they know it."

"All right. They say no. Then what do I do? Come home like a whipped hound?"

Bullard drew the secret portion of the orders out of his desk drawer and fondled its envelope thoughtfully.

"You will find the answer here," he said. "This will tell you all you need to know."

Bullard got up abruptly and walked to the window, where he stood for a moment looking out into the dim night, his hands clasped behind him. Benton saw that his fingers were twitching nervously, and was surprised, for he had seldom seen the celebrated captain of the *Pollux* display strong emotion. Then Bullard began speaking again, but still facing out the window. His tone was low and his voice solemn.

"Benton, lad, there is something I want you to remember when you get out there on Nestor. That is that I am sending you on this mission only because I am forbidden to take it myself. The darkest hours in any senior's life come when he is compelled to delegate a job so dirty that he would shrink from touching it himself. This job, Benton, is that kind of job. If the worst comes and you *have* to open this envelope, you will have no choice but comply with its harsh instructions. You will want to squirm out from under, you will want to rebel, you will hate me—"

"Oh, no, skipper," exclaimed Benton. "I can carry out orders. You know it!"

"To the letter, whatever the cost, whatever your opinion of the orders themselves or the man who wrote them?"

"Why, yes, sir. What proper officer would not?"

Bullard whirled, and Benton thought he caught a twinkle in his eyes, though the mouth still held its grim set.

"There have been times, Benton," Bullard said softly, with a faint smile, "when officers have not always adhered to the *letter*. In fact, on several such occasions I believe you acted as an accomplice." Then his face grew stern again, and the voice peremptory and commanding. "In this instance you are to attempt nothing of the sort. Orders are orders."

He handed Benton the sealed package. Then he shook him warmly by the hand. Benton looked so crestfallen that Bullard was beginning to wonder if he had not overplayed his hand.

"If you work things right," said Bullard, in a more confident tone, "you will bring this back unopened along with Grory. I cannot tell you in advance what my instructions are, but I assure you that I have prepared for every conceivable contingency. The only hints I can give you are these: be cool and civil; do not bluster or enter into a debate. But be bold, be confident when you make your demand. If it is refused, go back quietly to the ship and wait. If nothing happens by the expiration of four hours, then you will have to do what I have written here. Good luck!"

Many times on the trip out Benton took the mysterious envelope out of the safe and examined it hopefully. There was no clue to what it contained. As often he put it back, more curious than ever. His confidence in Bullard was unbounded; he was sure of one thing, and that was that those hidden orders *did* have the answer to anything that might come up. But what? Bullard had intimated that carrying them out would be distasteful, perhaps hazardous. Oh, well!

Benton went through the ship with a fine-toothed comb, looking for secret gadgets that might have been planted there. He found nothing. Whatever Bullard expected him to do was probably in the strictly Bullardian manner— a pulling of rabbits out of a hat. He was still puzzling over the teaser when the Trojan group showed up on his screen. A little later he was setting the newly christened *Texas Ranger* down on Nestor.

When he stepped out of the space lock he saw to his surprise that he had company. A Martian gunboat, bristling with long Zordich guns, lay to his left; a Saturnian sloop of war, studded with tube openings, lay to the right. An armed yacht, sporting the triple-cross emblem of the Trojans, was a little way ahead of where he lay. It was apparent that the denizens on the outer planets were not taking disarmament as seriously as the gullible Earth people. It was very disconcerting.

Then Benton thought of his orders inside in the safe. It bucked him up. No doubt the presence of these vessels was one of the contingencies that Bullard had provided for. Bullard was a careful man. Benton walked on toward the port.

His interview with the Boss of Nestor was short and to the point. He stated what he had come for; the answer was a curt no. That was all there was to it.

"Very well," said Benton, calmly. Bullard's words still rang in his ears—"be confident, be cool, be bold."

Someone in the audience chamber snickered, but Benton ignored it. He walked down the aisle and out the door with a firm step but without haste. At the door the Nestorian captain of the port who had escorted him to the palace took him back in tow.

"You take it easier than the marshals did," he said, in an offhand way. "They raved and swore. But it didn't get 'em anywhere. Our Boss is tough."

"Yeah?"

"Yes. Are you shoving off now?"

"Oh, no," said Benton. "I haven't finished yet."

They walked along for a hundred yards while the beetle-browed captain mulled that cryptic remark over. At length he asked for enlightenment.

"You came for Grory and the Boss said you couldn't have him? So what? Bluffs don't work on Nestor."

"I wouldn't know."

"Then what? What have you got up your sleeve?"

"You'll find out in just four hours from now—if I don't get Grory."

"Oh, a threat, huh?"

"Nope. A statement."

The port captain left Benton at his ship, then walked across to the Martian vessel and said something to its skipper. Then Benton saw him making his way toward the Saturnian. Benton called for his steward.

"Bring out that fancy deck chair we found in the cabin," he directed.

Ten minutes later Benton was stretched out in a luxurious silken chair over which a striped awning made a canopy against the weak Nestorian sun. By his side stood a taboret and on it a tall, cool drink. Benton relaxed. It was his way of displaying confidence.

Presently the Martian captain came over, read the name of his ship, looked enviously at the fancy chair layout, then opened the conversation.

"Sticking around awhile?"

"Dunno," said Benton. "That's up to the Boss. When I get Grory, I shove off."

The Martian asked several more questions, but the answers were vague and noncommittal. The conversation languished. Benton glanced at his watch. An hour had gone. He took a sip of his drink, closed his eyes and pretended to doze.

The Martian went away. Half an hour later Benton had a new visitor. It was Nestor's deputy Boss, a scarred, one-eyed ex-burglar named Fraggin.

"What's this about an ultimatum?" he demanded roughly. "Captain Zeeter said you said you were going to get Grory inside of four hours or else."

"He quoted me inaccurately, but that was the substance of it."

"Or else what?" Fraggin looked like he was about to swing.

"When the time limit expires I shall carry out the un-completed portion of my orders. That's all. What's in 'em is my business."

"Who wrote any such orders?" growled Fraggin.

"That's none of your business either, but I don't mind telling you. Bullard did—Admiral Bullard, Commandant of Lunar Base and captain of the *Pollux*. You ought to know him. He pulled the raid on Titania."

"Yeah, yeah, I know him," said Fraggin, rubbing one of his scars thoughtfully. There was not a man in all the Trojans that didn't know him. Most had been arrested by him at one time or another.

"Well," said Fraggin after a long and what must have been for him a painful silence, "I gotta be goin'!"

"Okay," said Benton serenely, reaching for his drink. "I'll be seeing you." Then he settled down to do some con-centrated, if well concealed, worrying. At that moment he would gladly have given a pair of fingers for some ad-vance knowledge of what that sealed envelope held. He felt that he should be making preparations, not dawdling in a silky chair. But he knew he was being watched intently from three ships, and now that he had chosen his role he must stick it out to the bitter end.

It still lacked ten minutes to the deadline when the squad of soldiers approached. Fraggin led them. Benton glanced up with a pretense of indifference, and then a great weight rolled off his soul. Struggling and cursing in the midst of the squad was the man Grory, handcuffed to the soldiers on either side of him. Benton turned his head and called the steward.

"Ask the master-at-arms to come out," he said. "Here comes our prisoner."

The exchange of formal papers took only a few minutes. Then the *Texas Ranger's* tubes began to glow and a little later she was in the void, headed home. Benton decided to while the time away by refreshening his astragation. Working out the sights made the days of the voyage pass quickly. Almost before he realized it, he was making his landing on Luna.

A prison van from Justice was there to meet him, and Benton took the receipt for Grory from an astonished-looking chief marshal. He declined to answer any questions, but the moment he was rid of his prisoner, he hurried over to the Administration Building.

"Well done," said Bullard, meeting him at the door. "I knew you could do it. Any trouble?"

"Not a bit," said Benton proudly, then to make the most of his brief spot in the limelight, produced the envelope still bearing its seals. "I didn't even have to use this, sir."

"Ah, splendid," said Bullard, taking it and dropping it in the drawer. "You may go back to your regular duties now, Benton, and thank you."

"Yes, sir, of course. But I *am* a little curious. You may not know it, sir, but I was worried. I'm itching to know what those orders were."

Bullard looked at him quizzically. Should he tell him? After all he had been put in an awful hole and had come through with flying colors. Bullard felt he rated something. He would have preferred that Benton never knew, but he had asked, and it was a request that was hard to deny.

"All right, Benton, here you are. Here is the shameful thing you might have had to do."

"Shameful?" said the amazed Benton, taking the envelope and pulling off its seals. Bullard watched him intently as he shook out the contents and fished through them. Benton had expected to find several pages of closely written instructions. Instead he found only sheets of blank paper. Then, in the middle, he found a little slip of paper on which were written three brief words.

"Great God!" he cried, as the enormity of it hit him. He stared at the terse sentence in frank disbelief. Then he laughed. The paper fluttered onto Bullard's desk where the three words lay until Bullard tore them into fine little bits. The words were:

RETURN TO BASE.

WORLD *Junior* LIBRARY

Exciting, action-filled, inspiring and always engross-
ing, WORLD JUNIOR LIBRARY books will delight
all boys and girls who love good reading. These are
quality books by famous authors, in handsome, cloth-
bound library editions.

TITLES NOW AVAILABLE

JILL'S VICTORY *by Elisa Bialk*
THE SUN-DOG TRAIL *by Jack London*
SMOKE BELLEW *by Jack London*
JEAN CRAIG GRADUATE NURSE
by Kay Lyttleton
PAT'S HARMONY *by Page Cooper*
GHOST GABLES *by Mildred A. Wirt*
THE PAINTED SHIELD *by Mildred A. Wirt*
WILD STALLION *by Bud Murphy*
BULLARD OF THE SPACE PATROL
by Malcolm Jameson
FAVORITE DOG STORIES
edited by Marguerite Bloch
COMANCHE *by David Appel*
MONKEY SHINES *by Earl S. Miers*

THE WORLD PUBLISHING COMPANY

CLEVELAND AND NEW YORK